TOO EARLY TO KNOW WHO'S WINNING

KARLA HUEBNER

Black Rose Writing | Texas

First printing

This is a work of fiction. Names, characters, businesses, places, events, and incidents are either the products of the author's imagination or used in a fictitious manner. Any resemblance to actual persons, living or dead, or actual events is purely coincidental.

ISBN: 978-1-68513-165-4
PUBLISHED BY BLACK ROSE WRITING
www.blackrosewriting.com

Printed in the United States of America
Suggested Retail Price (SRP) $21.95

Too Early to Know Who's Winning is printed in Bookman Old Style

*As a planet-friendly publisher, Black Rose Writing does its best to eliminate unnecessary waste to reduce paper usage and energy costs, while never compromising the reading experience. As a result, the final word count vs. page count may not meet common expectations.

In memory of Betty Dietz and Denise Minor,
both gone too soon.

TOO EARLY TO KNOW WHO'S WINNING

1

On Election Day, Jacobine Flaa was glancing through her email, which tended to accumulate. She deleted, unread, "I lost my teenage son to suicide" and "Robocall Update: We need actions, not empty promises" and opened at random another.

Wed, Nov 2, 2016, 9:04 AM

Dear Sir / Madam,

The world will be watching the United States on Tuesday 8th November as Hillary Clinton and Donald Trump's lengthy and expensive campaigns conclude with the election of the country's next President.

To mark the election of the next leader of one of the world's most powerful countries, we are offering our readers a 50% discount on four of our best-selling titles in the field of political science. Please click here to read more.

Jacobine deleted this as well, having no desire whatsoever to purchase political science titles, whether or not they might be categorizable in any sense as best-selling. She continued on.

Front-Page Election News: More Horserace,
More Trump, More Presidency
FAIR fair@fair.org
Fri, Nov 4, 2016, 5:45 PM

A FAIR analysis of front-page election
coverage in three major dailies revealed a
strong emphasis on horserace politics at the
expense of issue coverage. The study found a
lopsided focus on Donald Trump over Hillary
Clinton, and an overwhelming focus on the
presidential race at the expense of all other
electoral contests.

This information did not surprise her. After a time she
ceased either looking at or deleting emails since there was
only so much of this that one could do when one's in-box
alone typically contained over twenty-two thousand
messages. In any case, before long she was meeting two
friends for supper at a restaurant. Even on Election Day
one could not think constantly about the election,
especially if one had already voted, which Jacobine just
had. While she lived in a state that allowed early voting,
and she had considered taking advantage of this, she felt
an opposition to casting a ballot prior to any last-minute
surprises. If nothing else, it was always possible that
waiting until Election Day would result in her finally
looking up exactly who was running for school board and
city council, not to mention judges. It was not, however,
her normal practice to succeed in doing that. And so now
she ran a comb through her short dark hair, added an
infinity scarf for warmth and to dress up her plain top,
and set off.

At the restaurant, Kerry had arrived first but insisted she had not waited long. "I just got here, really. Cinda messaged that she's running a little late so we should go ahead and get a table."

They got their table, ordered drinks. It was one of those times when they examined the specialty cocktail menu and ordered from that; not a celebratory dinner but nonetheless a day not quite ordinary. They were both wearing "I voted" stickers.

"I suppose it's too early to know who's winning," said Kerry. "East coast polls are just now closing."

"Yes," said Jacobine.

"Do you think Hillary will win?"

"I think it's going to be a tight race."

"She's been polling pretty well."

"A lot of people seem to have turned against her, though. She's not that popular with Bernie supporters, and a lot of people don't like her because she's a Clinton."

"True," sighed Kerry. "But surely those people won't vote for Trump."

"They may stay home," said Jacobine.

"True," said Kerry. "Let's hope not."

They spoke of other things and were asked if they wanted another cocktail, so they ordered a second round.

"I wonder where Cinda is," said Kerry, pulling out her phone. "Maybe she's left another message."

There was no message.

"I'll text her," said Kerry. "I don't want to be out too late."

Jacobine swished her straw in her drink. The campaign against plastic straws had not yet begun, or if it had, she and Kerry were not yet aware of it. Nonetheless, Jacobine never used a plastic straw unless the waitstaff had already put one in her drink. She felt they were wasteful and she was no longer five years old, back when it was exciting to drink with a straw and most straws were still paper and might collapse in mid-suck.

"She says she's on her way," reported Kerry. "She's parking the car."

"Oh," said Jacobine, unimpressed.

"Here you are!" exclaimed Cinda, appearing above them. "So sorry to be late, I was meeting with my financial planner."

"Welcome," said Kerry.

"Hi," said Jacobine.

"Sit down, we're on our second round," said Kerry. "Here's the drink menu."

"I'm trying to figure out my retirement," said Cinda. "I had to meet with my planner to update my investments and look at my tiny pensions from my various jobs and all that. Jacobine, do you have a financial planner?"

"No," said Jacobine.

"You should probably have one. When do you think you'll retire?"

"Well, I suppose probably around the time when Social Security will let me." She elaborated on the options and constraints relating to her birthdate and Social Security's rising "full retirement" age.

"Yeah, but your job doesn't pay into Social Security."

"No, but I need to maximize my pension since I won't have been there that long, so I use the Social Security timing as a guide."

"I might retire at sixty-two, if I can swing it," said Cinda. "The question is whether I can. The planner has to do some more work for me on this."

Kerry was about fifteen years younger, so her interest in retirement was more theoretical and she offered no comments on the subject. She would also have a much larger pension than Jacobine, assuming that nothing destroyed it in the next twenty years or so. In the United States in 2016, it was not possible to make assumptions about whether a pension would still exist in twenty years, although one had to make such assumptions at the same time as recognizing them to be entirely hypothetical. Assumptions about Social Security were equally hypothetical, although it could be expected that large contingents of the population, on all parts of the political spectrum, would rise up and protest if Social Security were actually to be taken away.

"I'm so fed up with my job," said Cinda. "My new boss is clueless. He calls meetings and then spends them looking at his cell phone."

The waitress arrived and took Cinda's drink order, and Kerry and Jacobine indicated that within moments they would want to order food.

"There are some tempting jobs out there," observed Cinda. "I'm considering applying for some of them. Of course, they have to be in locations that interest me, too. I'd really like to get something in the western part of the country."

"What about someplace like Vermont?" said Kerry.

"Oh, I wouldn't say no to Vermont," said Cinda. "Or even Crystal Bridges in Arkansas. I want to be someplace with good hiking. The hiking around here is simply uninspiring. I'm a western gal at heart, I want mountains, I want white-water rafting."

"We're a bit short on mountains here, it's true," said Jacobine.

"Oh my god, it's practically flat as a pancake here," said Cinda. "It's so monotonous."

"It's hilly where you live, though," said Kerry. "Not mountainous, of course, but seriously hilly."

"I *live* on a hill," confirmed Cinda. "And whenever it rains, the streets downhill are flooded and I have to take an alternate route to get to work."

"Not quite flat as a pancake," observed Jacobine.

"My neighborhood is so dull," continued Cinda. "It's not nearly as nice as my old neighborhood. And now with the election, it's full of Trump signs."

Kerry shook her head sadly. "My neighborhood has some too."

"Yeah, there are a couple in my neighborhood as well," said Jacobine.

"My neighborhood has more than just *some*," said Cinda. "All of a sudden they sprouted up like mushrooms. They're everywhere. Can you believe it? Who on earth in their right mind... Well, I'm sure a lot of Republicans will be staying home or voting for Hillary, because Trump isn't even a real Republican. He doesn't stand for any of their values. He's just a windbag. Full of hot air."

"Do you really think Republican voters will stay home because of Trump?" said Kerry with some skepticism.

"Not all of them, no, of course not," said Cinda. "Look at our sheep-flock neighbors with the Trump signs. But as I say, he doesn't stand for the things Republicans tend to stand for, plus he's a scandal-laden misogynistic multiple bankrupt."

The waitress brought Cinda's drink, and Kerry and Jacobine ordered supper while Cinda examined the menu and asked about various options.

"I think I'll have the chicken," she said at last, "I'm starving and it sounds so yummy. I'm so glad to hear that you don't use Amish chicken. Everyone thinks the Amish are so quaint but they're terrible to their livestock. To them their livestock are just like widgets, it's all about profit. Animal welfare means nothing to them."

The waitress made no comment on Amish chicken but merely promised to put their orders in immediately.

"This is such a nice place," said Cinda. "I'm so glad you thought of coming here, Kerry. I always enjoy seeing what's new on the menu. And this drink is fabulous. I've already forgotten what's in it, but the elderflower and fresh mint are very nice touches." She smoothed her freshly de-grayed shades of blonde and swiveled to admire the décor, which in this room involved walls painted a deep aqua.

"It's one of my favorite downtown restaurants," said Kerry. "Their mac-and-cheese is to die for."

"I looked at that," said Jacobine, "but they put breadcrumbs on it."

"You could ask them to leave off the breadcrumbs," said Cinda.

"I'd rather order something I don't make at home," said Jacobine. "I make my macaroni and cheese with whatever kind of cheese is in the refrigerator, and then I slice peppers into it."

"I love the breadcrumbs," said Kerry. "So good."

"As far as I'm concerned, they're as bad as croutons on a salad," said Jacobine. "Just wrong. But we're all different."

"I'm thinking of applying for this job in Jackson Hole," said Cinda. "I would love to live in Jackson Hole."

"What's the job?"

"They have a museum of Wildlife Art there. It's an interesting possibility. It could be a nice job to wind down my career with; it's not full time, so I'd have lots of time to take the doggies hiking and do stained glass."

"Can you afford a job like that?" inquired Kerry.

"Isn't Jackson Hole expensive?" said Jacobine.

"Well, I wouldn't say Jackson Hole is as affordable as here, but there's pretty much nowhere in the country that's as affordable as here. If you want to live someplace cheaper than here and have a halfway decent quality of life, you'd have to move to Mexico or someplace like that."

"One of my friends retired to Mexico," said Jacobine. "She seems to like it there."

"Where?" inquired Kerry.

"The Yucatán."

"I don't want to move to Mexico," said Cinda. "It's too hot there and my Spanish is minimal."

"Well, I don't want to move to Mexico either," said Jacobine, "for pretty much the same reasons as you, but it's an option for some people."

"Mexico has all that drug crime, too," asserted Cinda. "Drug lords killing people right and left, and corrupt police."

"I don't think that's particularly typical of the Yucatán," said Jacobine. "Probably the crime in Mexico is specific to particular areas, just like it is here."

"Drug crime is spread all over the US," said Cinda. "Look at meth and opioids."

"Yes, but not everyone in the US is directly endangered by drug lords having shootouts, and the same is probably true of Mexico."

"Well, I'm not moving to Mexico, so the point is moot," said Cinda. "The climate here is unpleasant enough without moving somewhere that's even hotter and muggier."

"Did you ever get that wood stove that you were interested in?" Kerry asked, as a possible change of topic.

"No, I've been vacillating about which one to get," said Cinda. "And it's getting late in the season, it's already November, and I'd like to have one installed so that I can enjoy it!" She began to describe three different models of wood stove in minute detail. "I'm really eager to decide on the wood stove now that I've put the new tile floor in that room. I can see I'm going to want to spend a lot of time in that room now that I've remodeled it, so getting the stove is key. Unless I go with a gas fireplace unit instead. I've also been looking into those."

"Do you have a preference between wood and gas?" asked Jacobine.

"Well..." said Cinda before ruminating at length about both. "Mainly I want to get something installed now before the cold weather really hits. It's November, after all. I just had my furnace checked. You should be sure to get your furnaces checked if you haven't already. By November the furnace people are getting booked up."

"Yes..." said Jacobine.

"In fact, it's already Election Day!" exclaimed Cinda.

"Yes..." agreed Kerry and Jacobine.

"Have you heard anything about the returns yet? I don't think I can bear to check yet."

"East Coast polls closed a while ago, or at least most of them did," said Kerry, pulling out her phone. "Midwest polls in Central Time are closing."

"Hillary will win, of course," said Cinda, "but it could be tight because of the swing states and the Electoral College. I'm not sure I want to follow the returns closely, my life is stressful enough without that."

"You're sure Hillary will win?" said Kerry.

"She's got to," said Cinda. "I mean, look at her competition."

"Yes, but the media doesn't cover her very well," persisted Kerry. "Trump gives them a circus. They can't resist covering his antics 24/7. And people keep throwing dirt at Hillary. Even if most of it's not real dirt, it turns people against her."

Jacobine said, "I've talked to people who say they don't know what to do because they don't like either candidate."

"Well, it ought to be a no-brainer, because no matter what your politics, Hillary is a better option than Trump," said Cinda. "He's an incompetent, inexperienced idiot, whereas she's experienced and competent."

"Yeah, but lots of people don't like that she's competent," said Jacobine. "They figure any politician with any experience must be corrupt."

"There's some truth to that, but look at the Obamas," said Cinda. "Hugely popular and not a whiff of scandal attached to either one."

"Not popular with the GOP, though," said Kerry. "Look how they kept blocking everything Obama tried to do."

"Popular with the electorate, though," said Cinda. "Hillary will win, it's just going to be a nail-biter if the early returns are any indication."

"I'm not so sure," said Jacobine.

"Well, she'd better win!"

"Of course," returned Jacobine, "because we're fucked if she doesn't."

"Deep doo-doo indeed," said Cinda.

"This is so nerve-wracking," said Kerry. "I really, really want to assume that things will be okay, but what if they aren't? Trump has so much news coverage and all we hear about Hillary is this crap about her emails."

They contemplated this a moment.

"I've decided to repaint my living room," announced Cinda. "I thought the color I'd chosen would work, but I think the store mixed the paint wrong. It's not the same as when I've bought that color in the past."

"Do you mean in your old house? You know it's not going to look the same, because the lighting isn't the same."

"It's demonstrably a different color. I'm going to have the store remix so that I can try again."

Jacobine took her straw and pounded meditatively at the remaining ice cubes in her drink, and their food came.

At home that night, Jacobine turned her laptop to live election coverage, but for the most part ignored it. She was tired and turned off the lights, but left the laptop on at low volume. As she dozed in and out of wakefulness, she heard that Hillary Clinton had called Donald Trump to concede. She sat up and closed the laptop.

2

It was just unbelievable—how on earth could any nation have freely elected Donald Trump president? Not that he'd got more votes. But the vote was to all intents and purposes split between Clinton and Trump. Why any working-class person would believe that a narcissistic demagogue pseudo-billionaire, with multiple bankruptcies and a history of stiffing those he owed, might actually bother to do anything to benefit them... It was just mind-boggling.

The outpouring of fear and despair following the election was intense, yet Jacobine's several Trump-voting relatives didn't seem to get why people were so upset; they evidently thought Democrats were just sore losers. But people were already afraid, even this early, because Trump was not just an unpredictable bully and narcissist, but he'd attracted a base that included the KKK and a host of other active bigots who now felt emboldened to come out of the woodwork to publicly taunt and threaten anyone who seemed nonwhite or nonheterosexual.

Jacobine's cousin Sam said, "I'm terrified. I'm terrified for a whole raft of reasons. I'm self-employed with a pre-existing condition, so I'm terrified that I'll lose my health insurance. I'm also terrified that Trump will piss off ISIS and they'll bomb DC. And I'm terrified that if I show up at a public protest, I'll be beaten up by Trump's thugs. I recognize that I'm a coward; I've always known it, and this is part of why I have such a deep admiration for people who were in the Resistance during World War II. But basically, I have to stop paying attention to the news to retain my sanity."

"I hope I'm wrong and that Trump will do some good things," said Jacobine, "but I'm not optimistic. I didn't see any signs during the campaign that he'll rise to the occasion."

Jacobine's History Department colleague Beth, a medievalist, said, "I am so freaked out and depressed! I'm going to have to avoid Facebook and the news in order to be able to work."

Jacobine didn't consider herself brave—she figured she couldn't know how she would react in various situations. She told Beth, "I do feel a generalized mild depression and anxiety, but I plan to attend tonight's protest downtown. I think I'm in a good position to speak up in small ways. I recognize that Trump was legally elected according to the laws of the United States, so my goal is to hold him accountable and prevent him from enacting harmful changes. I hope he'll surprise me with some good deeds but I'm not expecting it."

> Protest this evening
> Jacobine Flaa <flaa.di.dah@gmail.com>
> Fri, Nov 11, 2016, 1:23 PM
> to Kerry
>
> Hi Kerry,

I saw on Facebook that you too are interested in this evening's protest. I plan to go—want to meet up?

I'm about to go out and run some errands, but should be home by four or so and accessible by phone or email.

Jacobine

There was no response from Kerry, so Jacobine walked downtown by herself. At the gathering, there were some speeches, various signs, reasonable attendance for a medium-sized city. As the event broke up, Jacobine noticed her neighbor Suzanne DuPre preparing to walk home with a friend, so she joined them.

"I was a little afraid the Trump supporters might be out looking for a fight," said the friend. "They scare me."

"Yeah, I wondered about that too," said Jacobine. "That's why I wore these heavy snow boots—I can kick with them but they also wouldn't have fallen off if I'd had to run in them."

"That's smart," said Suzanne. "I didn't think about wearing anything protective. After all, it's normally pretty safe downtown. Still, I was relieved not to see gangs of MAGA-hatters. It's been kind of unsettling to see some of our neighbors support Trump."

"Yes, but I don't think it's really too surprising," said Jacobine. "We knew our neighborhood had a political mix, it's just that politics aren't seen as an appropriate topic for the email list and the socials."

"I suppose that's true," said Suzanne. "Still, I was horrified when Deb Dowd came out as a Trump campaigner. She's always been so friendly and she helped me learn how to train for the 5K and longer races."

"She's friendly," agreed Jacobine, "and she's good at organizing social events and that kind of thing, but all the same I've always thought there was something off about her. I wasn't that surprised when she started spouting conspiracy theory weirdness at meetings and just not even making sense when she gets going on her wacko topics. She starts rambling into completely disconnected craziness."

"I guess I do remember her going wild about some loony complaint about the fire department once," said Suzanne. "It made no sense whatsoever."

"Exactly, she was practically frothing at the mouth about this imaginary problem. I think that's around the time people began discouraging her from attending the meetings. She would take up five or ten minutes raving."

"I had no idea," said Suzanne. "I guess I only happened to be there for the one time when she went off on the fire department."

"Greg Stevenson told me the other right-wing neighbors think she makes them look bad because she can be so nutty."

"That's so sad," said Suzanne. "I thought of her as something close to a friend. I won't stop training with her, but I don't feel comfortable hanging out much with Trump supporters, especially crazy ones."

• • •

A few days later, Jacobine found an email from Kerry.

Kerry Baker <BakerKerryJoy@gmail.com>
Mon, Nov 14, 2016, 10:07 AM

Hi Jacobine—

Sorry I missed you... I took a break from email
and news this weekend (and was out of town
Friday night).
Hope it was a good time!

Thanks—
Kerry

Jacobine Flaa <flaa.di.dah@gmail.com>
Mon, Nov 14, 2016, 10:46 AM
to Kerry

Hi Kerry,

The protest was pretty well attended and remained
peaceful, so all was good.

Jacobine

3

Pearl Harbor Day arrived, and the weather turned wintry. Jacobine felt a general sense of melancholy and anxiety about the future. More and more white supremacists were being chosen for the national government, and reports of hate crimes and hateful behavior multiplied. Jacobine tried not to focus on the news, but nonetheless felt it was wrong and foolish to ignore the dangerous direction the US was currently headed. She couldn't help feeling the US was on the path of Nazi Germany.

These feelings sometimes made it hard to concentrate on her work, which involved a combination of teaching in the local university's History Department and helping manage its museum. Her research focused on Public History and on the experience of America's immigrants during the nineteenth and early twentieth centuries; in the museum, she curated exhibitions and worked with interns from her department's Public History track. Her work in the university museum was, in fact, part of how she had gotten to know Kerry and Cinda; Kerry was a printmaker in the Art Department who had helped her curate a show of WPA women printmakers, while Cinda was employed at a small art museum about an hour distant.

●　●　●

On Facebook, Jacobine wrote: *It snowed a little last night. I think it's time to give up on my pepper plants*. During the day, it was just above freezing; the snow had turned to rain. She walked over to the local movie theater, but the streets were dreary, and a man who passed her on the sidewalk turned around to follow her. She had known immediately upon seeing him that he was going to do that; and then, when she turned to look, there he was. It was odd being able to predict such things, but sometimes you just knew, picked up on cues. She didn't feel endangered because it was, after all, only seven o'clock and there were bars and restaurants open and some traffic and other pedestrians, but it kept her from pausing to see whether anything along the way to the theater was interesting, which was annoying. Before long, though, he lost interest and drifted away.

Interracial couples were arriving for the bio-pic *Loving*, which told the story of how Richard Loving and Mildred Jeter, who had married in Washington, DC, in 1958, fought for the right to live as a legally married couple in the state of Virginia, and how they eventually won their case in 1967. Afterward, Jacobine concluded it was a good enough movie. Not perhaps cinematically remarkable, but certainly worth seeing, because it did a good job of telling an important and moving story. She had heard of the Lovings before but not realized they were a working-class rural couple. Educated urban people perhaps had more of a reputation for going against custom, but working-class people also had a long history of not conforming to the expectations of the bourgeoisie. However, it was perhaps less common for working-class families to take their civil rights cases to the Supreme Court, as the Lovings had done with the help of the ACLU. She was glad that their story was being told to new generations.

There was growing interest in putting pressure on the Electoral College, especially as recounts of questionable votes seemed stalled. Jacobine didn't see how the Electoral College could do other than vote as the rules dictated— she doubted that there would be more than a handful of electors, if that, who voted their conscience instead. And one couldn't expect otherwise. Both candidates had gone in knowing that they had to win the electoral vote rather than (or along with, normally) the popular vote. Still, Jacobine was all for protesting and showing mass dissatisfaction with the Electoral College's existence, and making clear that Trump didn't have a mandate.

She wrote:

We must do what we can to retain democracy and fairness before and after the inauguration. Trump's choices for advisors are absolutely insane. White supremacists, climate change deniers, anti-educationists, on and on. It's important for as many of us as can to make ourselves heard so that maybe these thugs will think twice before locking us up. If we're out in force protesting, they can't beat all of us up. Not everyone feels able to be brave at present, so those of us who are able need to step up. I don't feel brave, but I'm angry—I will join and not be silent. I have a job, no children to support, and can leave the country if necessary, so I can speak out in place of those who are too afraid. I need to send contributions to the organizations that are fighting this dictator-to-be and his mob.

The news generally was so appalling that Jacobine felt depressed listening to it driving to and from work. Syrian refugees, ISIS attacks, Al Qaeda, misogynists, white supremacists, rogue police killing black people—any place full of people seemed like a potential target for the bloodthirsty.

•   •   •

In mid-December Jacobine bought her Christmas tree and began to maneuver it into position in her living room, but discovered that she needed new Christmas lights because for some reason only half the lights on one string would glow. She thought she'd just dash to the hardware store and come right back, but this errand took much longer than expected, because President Obama was giving a press conference and she felt obliged to listen to the whole thing before getting out of the car.

Jacobine had never cared much for his speaking style—she felt that while President Obama was very articulate, he broke up the flow of his sentences too much and often sounded affectless. His phrasing in the press conference was cautious, which on some questions seemed suitable and on others unfortunate. Jacobine wanted to hear more resistance to Trump's demagoguery and ties to Vladimir Putin. Still, President Obama made clear, at least, that he thought Putin was behind the Russian efforts to sway the election in Trump's favor, and he emphasized that fake news—the brand new term for disinformation—became believable to people when they'd been hearing similar things from the real news and from the Republican party.

She felt the president kept his temper well. After all, the legitimate media had played into Trump's agenda. Despite many reporters' disdain for Trump, they had not done the necessary investigative reporting and had instead wasted time fussing over Hillary Clinton's email server as if that were truly important, as if Clinton as Secretary of State had handled her email any differently than earlier officials in similar positions.

And so Jacobine returned home to try to focus on decorating her Christmas tree, but it was hard not to become teary about the news. The radio now informed her that parents of transgender children were hastening to ask to change their children's identity on government documents in case the Trump administration decided to rescind that possibility.

Holiday pleasures, and indeed even the final papers and exams and museum work that had to be wrapped up by the end of the semester, seemed like something from another world.

4

As Hillary Clinton had gained more of the popular vote whereas Donald Trump had secured the states needed to win the Electoral College, anticipation continued to run high regarding the electoral vote. Only three other such elections had occurred since 1824, and with evidence of Russian interference in this election, as well as other evidences of irregularity, there was now significant hope that some electors might vote to reflect conscience rather than their official choice. Occasional "faithless electors" had voted against party in the past, although this had not changed the final result since the election of 1796. As it was unlikely that a significant number of electors would switch, feelings were strong that the Electoral College, created in distrust of the uneducated masses, had outlived its purpose.

"Yesterday we were stunned, today we organize!" said emails. "Add your name: Abolish the Electoral College," urged petitions; Jacobine signed.

Plans for protests were announced. "We go into this with sober expectations. Barring an extraordinary event, the Electoral College will likely elect Donald Trump as president. However, we can achieve two concrete things with these protests even if Trump wins the vote."

She read:

Trump's razor-thin victories in battleground states were made possible in part by massive voter suppression. 2016 was the first general election without the full protection of the Voting Rights Act. Over 800 polling places were closed. Early voting was cut. Restrictive voter ID laws were in effect. Hundreds of thousands of voters—disproportionately people of color—were purged from the voter rolls.

As the Electoral College vote approached, the emails increased.

The bigger the crowds and media attention when Electors go to every state capitol on Monday Dec. 19 to cast their votes, the better equipped they will be to do the right thing and do the will of the people—and the more we'll debunk Trump's claim of a 'mandate' after he lost the popular vote and was helped by Russia.

Likewise, emails pointed out that "Before they vote, the electors need to know how Russia influenced the election."

Jacobine lived only an hour from her state capital, so she RSVP'd to attend and protest. She felt fortunate that her work schedule was sufficiently flexible that it was possible for her to take a Monday morning off; obviously that would not be the case for most of the working population. No one else she knew was going to the Capitol. Neither Kerry nor Cinda could go.

It being mid-December now, she suited up in her old ski gear and a pair of snow boots, pinning a sign to the back of her coat to keep her hands free. She worried that it might be hard to park near the Capitol, but there proved to be a large garage under the building.

The weather was cold and icy. Protesters gradually gathered, many with large signs. A few leaders with megaphones began to give instructions regarding how the group would march around the Capitol and how to address the electors as they filed in. The morning grew long as Jacobine and the others marched and chanted, while relatively little traffic drove past the Capitol to honk in support or to gesture disapproval.

Ultimately seven electors nationally defected, which was the largest number to do so in any American election of the past hundred years, but only two defected from Trump while five abandoned Clinton for other candidates. Three electors voted for Colin Powell, while John Kasich, Ron Paul, Bernie Sanders, and Faith Spotted Eagle each received one vote. Three additional electors who voted against their Clinton pledge found their votes invalidated according to local statutes; they were replaced or forced to vote again. And so the defections fell far short of the number needed to change the result of the election; thirty-five defections were needed in order to force a run-off vote in Congress.

5

Jacobine's neighborhood was holding its holiday social at a local pub. Her neighborhood was known for its frequent social events, which were planned by a Social Committee and intended to build rapport, encourage neighborhood safety, and also to attract new and desirable residents, augmenting the work of the Parks & Greenways Committee and the Garden Tour Committee. Jacobine approved of these aims and attended some medium percentage of the events each year, although she had yet to experience any truly memorable conversations at them. The young couples and the pairs of parents tended all to know one another, as did those who had grown up in the city and retired there. Jacobine generally found herself querying the elderly about the progress of their stroke rehabilitation, exchanging gardening chat with retired divorcees, or answering questions about her job to members of the Social Committee. Sometimes she brought Cinda along, because Cinda always enjoyed the socials and had once won third prize at the annual lasagna contest. However, Cinda now lived far enough away, closer to her job, that it was not very practical for her to go to evening events in Jacobine's neighborhood. Cinda often opined that she loved Jacobine's neighborhood but could not see herself living there because the yards were too small and it was not feasible to walk her dogs for an hour or two each day on such a limited number of residential streets. Kerry, meanwhile, thought Jacobine's neighborhood was very cute, but she did not attend its socials because her own neighborhood was equally cute in its different way and had events of its own, most of which Kerry did not have time free to attend anyway.

Jacobine hoped that the holiday social would put her in a more cheerful mood, but she recognized that her tendency was to attend these socials yet nonetheless feel mildly isolated and bored and uninclined to talk—which made her ask why she went if she wasn't going to engage socially. It was not for the food and drink, although these did make for a sometimes pleasant change from her own cooking. On this occasion, she ruminated that she did like many of her neighbors, even some who supported Trump. It could be important to go and make clear that most Americans had much in common and should not hate each other even if they hated each other's politics.

Indeed, the Christmas social proved pleasant enough and Jacobine was a little less restless than usual. Greg Stevenson confided feeling out of sorts—she had never been quite sure where he stood politically, but now he lamented and wondered how anyone could possibly have seen fit to vote for Trump. Judy Stone, who still had Trump signs in her yard, remained an otherwise normal, reasonable person to hang out with. Suzanne DuPre, who had gone to the anti-Trump rally after the election, didn't mention politics to Jacobine since the two had already determined that they were on the same side. With Terry Miller, the chair of the Social Committee, Jacobine agreed that the neighborhood usually functioned as a space of unity rather than as a divisive space, so perhaps it could continue to do so.

The city she presently lived in was, she supposed, much like the more western Midwestern city of her forebears—settlers who had come in the nineteenth century and stayed, and most of their descendants had stayed too. Numerous other people had come and gone as well—relative wanderers like Jacobine, Kerry, and Cinda, who went where they found work—but the area had a strong rootedness unlike most places Jacobine had lived. It was a little strange for her, but it was also familiar, as her extended family was deeply rooted in the area where their immigrant ancestors had settled, back in the days of Manifest Destiny.

At this particular social, Jacobine found herself experiencing an unexpected sense of disappointment at being single. It was surprising because, as she approached sixty, she rarely thought about that much anymore. Her family had long since ceased expecting her to marry, and her last breakup had occurred some years before her menopause. Besides, her hormones no longer filled her with ceaseless lust. It was true that she missed having a certain kind of male but not overly masculine energy around. Still, on this occasion her mild longing for a partner felt less sexual than sociological; it would have been pleasant to be accompanied by some nice and nicely dressed fellow, with whom she could make little jokes now and then and whom she could introduce, then let loose to forage among the hors d'oeuvres. Partners past had not taken on this role, nor had she expected them to, but for the moment she felt this lack of a conventional spouse. For that matter, a less conventional same-sex spouse would have served the same purpose and would have been equally acceptable to the neighbors who attended these socials. But spouse she had none.

6

The next day, Jacobine stopped at a local antique mall to see if there were any promising gifts to be found there, but she soon found herself feeling strangely melancholy amidst these castoffs, many of them from her own lifetime rather than technically antique, items someone else might have made witty use of but which were not of interest or pleasure for her. She did visit this particular antique mall now and then, and had occasionally found something to buy, but for the most part she did not have the energy to comb through the various stalls in search of real prizes, besides which she seemed to have reached an age at which she no longer felt like acquiring much. So at first she was not too surprised to feel a little down as she wandered the aisles, but the feeling grew stronger and remained even for a while after she had left the antique mall, causing her to wonder what could be prompting this sensation, or if there was some sad ghost haunting the antique mall.

Indeed, Jacobine found it hard to believe that Christmas was so near. Yes, she had a Christmas tree up and decorated. Yes, there was Christmas music on the radio. Yes, she'd received some Christmas cards already. No, she hadn't sent any cards yet. No, she hadn't bought her holiday groceries yet. No, she hadn't done any holiday cleaning. And she wasn't living in a place where it was especially fun to do Christmas shopping for her family, especially now that her mother had pretty much everything she needed and often read from a Kindle rather than buying new physical books.

Still, at least her mother was pretty active for her age. Some months back, Jacobine's mother had gone on a regime of taking turmeric pills thrice a day, which had apparently resulted in better mobility and greatly increased energy, to the extent that the doctor had told her to keep it up. Of late her mother had been going for short walks and had gone to Macy's on her own and done sundry other things, which was excellent, but all the same did not provide any clues as to what might make a welcome Christmas gift.

And then, as she looked over her bookshelves in search of something to read, Jacobine was painfully aware that she must own hundreds of books that she'd never read and was tempted to clear out. The idea of getting rid of books felt like a sign of impending death for a person with a history of collecting and saving stuff. For someone else, that might not be at all the case, but for herself, it was disturbing. She felt she should read a book at least once before deciding to get rid of it. And one got pleasant surprises, as when she'd finally read Nicholson Baker's *Vox*, which had proved enchanting even though about phone sex. Such a delightful book and far superior to the several volumes of erotica that people had given her in the nineties, which while well enough written had proved a complete turnoff. Those, she thought, she could readily discard.

7

On New Year's Eve, the radio offered a TED talk on happiness. Supposedly, people who let their minds wander were unhappier because they let their minds wander onto their worries. Jacobine found herself unimpressed with this hypothesis. Sure, it was good to be fully present in an activity, and one could practice being more present, but in Jacobine's opinion one also needed to let the mind wander. Creativity required a wandering as well as a focused mind. And if, for instance, she was driving and thinking mainly about what she saw alongside the road, was that being mindful because she was focused on the moment, or was that being distracted because she wasn't focused on the act of driving? And if she was putting laundry into the washer, it was true that she took pleasure in easily performing a necessary task, but she wasn't strongly focused on it and there were many things she'd enjoy more.

She supposed that while her life was not short of anxieties and feelings of melancholy about the future, on the whole she was a fairly happy soul who took pleasure in a great many things. She was not going to fret about whether she was experiencing happiness in the manner suggested by the TED talk. And so she read for a while and then went to bed.

With the new year, Jacobine was reminded that many people made an annual practice of making resolutions. She had no idea whether any of her friends did this, but in the first days of January, the radio and newspaper and internet were always full of stories about resolutions and whether it was actually useful to resolve to lose weight or exercise more or stop smoking. Jacobine occasionally read or listened to such stories, being curious what other humans cared about and whether that changed over the years, but she rarely made resolutions of her own. For 2017, thoughts drifted unasked through her mind of resolutions about more diligently bagging the fallen leaves in her yard, or even about making progress in sorting and filing her papers, but these were uninspiring. The idea of making resolutions to plant more vegetables or to publish more scholarly articles seemed almost equally pointless; such things did not really require making resolutions. Still, she thought that perhaps she could resolve to have a productive year and continue to resist Trump's incoming regime.

Venturing outdoors on New Year's Day, she discovered a yard sign leaning against her front door. It welcomed neighbors in English, Spanish, and Arabic, so she promptly installed it in the front yard. Later, when she walked to a nearby café, she was disappointed to see that hardly any other yards displayed this sign—Suzanne DuPre and her husband's house was the only location whose inhabitants Jacobine could identify, and only four other houses along her path displayed the sign—but perhaps not everyone in the neighborhood had opened the front door yet and found one, or maybe the signs had only been distributed to likely households; she wouldn't have been surprised if Suzanne herself had distributed them. In any case, Jacobine felt strongly that at a time when hate crimes were increasing post-election, and immigrants were feeling threatened, it was important to proclaim her support of immigrants and peaceful Muslims.

Indeed, as a historian whose research focused on the immigrant experience, Jacobine took considerable interest in the current situation of immigrants and ways in which residents reacted to them. She had been more accustomed to thinking about immigrants of the late nineteenth and early twentieth centuries—the period of massive European immigration, when Germans, Italians, Scandinavians, Russian Jews, and so many other groups had flooded in, often encouraged by the American railroad companies and by the promise of homesteads in the Midwest. And then there was the period of the Armenian diaspora resulting from the Armenian genocide, and the opening up of Asian immigration to the US. But she also paid attention to more recent migrations, especially, of late, the exodus of Syrians and others across the Mediterranean to Europe, desperate migrants who so often were drowning in the sea or finding themselves rejected once in Europe.

8

Although Jacobine had ended up on numerous email lists in recent years consequent to her small donations to various conservation and human rights organizations, she was relatively ill-informed about exactly what was going on with the Women's March that was planned for the day after the Trump inauguration. She knew that there was going to be a March, and she was all in favor, but the specifics were not foremost in her mind. She had a vague awareness that some of the marchers were knitting pink Pussy Hats to wear in protest against Trump's claim that he could freely grab women by the pussy; however, while she knew how to knit, she had not knitted anything in at least ten years, and she was not over fond of the color pink, so it did not occur to her that she might want to make a Pussy Hat even though the instructions were readily available online. Likewise, she knew that some people were going to be bussing and carpooling to Washington if they were not attending local iterations of the March, but she had no idea whether anyone she knew was among those planning to go to Washington. Consequently, she let the entire matter drift in her mind as something she was in favor of and might even participate in but about which she felt no energy to make actual plans. This was how she often approached things that did not relate to her professional life or, for that matter, her at this point nonexistent romantic life.

As the new semester began and the inauguration approached, she thought more about the upcoming March and felt more strongly that it could be a good thing to go to Washington for it. Nonetheless, she still had no clear sense of which people in her life were planning to be there. Kerry and Cinda thought they might perhaps attend local gatherings, but likewise did not express firm plans. December and early January seemed difficult times to make plans with people, what with holiday preparations and recovery from same. Jacobine's cousin Sam lived in DC, which meant that if she went, she would not have to stay in a hotel, which meant too that she could further put off making a decision. It was a day's drive for her to reach the city, so all she would have to do was arrange her work schedule. That was possible in this instance; she had only a morning meeting to attend that Friday, inauguration day.

As Jacobine drove, she gave little thought to the inauguration festivities, although she listened to reports on the radio. $107 million had been provided by wealthy donors, twice what any previous inauguration committee had raised and well beyond the cost of the events; and for years to come, questions would be asked about what had become of the excess cash. In the inaugural address, she heard Trump speak of "American carnage" and a "land of abandoned factories, economic angst, rising crime." As the United States was actually in economic recovery from the crash of 2008, unemployment was officially significantly below average, and violent crime was generally low, she and other listeners around the world were unimpressed by this apocalyptic fantasy. Later, it was even rumored that former Republican president Bush the younger had described Trump's speech as "some weird shit."

Arriving at her cousin's after dark, she learned that the inauguration crowds had been sparse and protests were erupting. Most of the protesting was peaceful, but anarchists had allegedly set fire to a limousine, and over two hundred people were arrested and charged with rioting.

The Women's March the next day, which she and Sam attended, was quite a different matter. The two of them pinned signs to their coats, charged their camera batteries and filled water bottles, and set off on the Metro to Union Station, where they ate a diner-style breakfast amid other arrivees and then began to walk, slowly but with a sense of excited purpose, toward the area where they understood people to be gathering initially. As they departed the station, they could see clumps of other marchers pausing to photograph one another and admire each other's signage and costuming. "We Are the Noisy Majority," said one sign; "Trust Women," said another; "Make America Empathize Again," said a third.

Getting nearer the official starting point, they could see an enormous mass of people occupying the entire street and all of the sidewalks. Pussy hats in every imaginable shade of pink could be seen, some of them very imaginatively done in more than one tint and texture, so that there might be a band of magenta angora giving panache to a hat of coral wool, or cables might have been added to the basic rib knit. And many, of course, were not wearing pussy hats at all, but went bareheaded, or wore pink cowboy hats with pink cat ears added, or wore caps and berets of other colors from subdued to fantastical, like the stars-and-stripes hat in the shape of a gesturing hand, or the diadems based on the Statue of Liberty's seven-rayed crown. There were bands and groups of drummers here and there playing spirited music.

Signs read, "Women's Rights Are Human Rights," "Our Bodies, Our Minds, Our Power," "I'm Not a Sore Loser, I'm an Informed Citizen."

And "Baltimore Women United," "Ohio Women for Climate Justice," "Michigan Women United in Diversity," "Portland Raging Grannies," and many other geographically specific signs.

The crowd was ethnically and religiously diverse, and signage emphasized this: Jacobine saw signs saying "Respect Women of Color," "Black Lives Matter," "Marching for Muslim Americans," "Ni Putas, Ni Santas, Solo Mujeres," and "Respete mi Existencia," as well as a family of Utah Mormons putting signs on the baby's stroller.

There were references to cats—"Pussy Grabs Back," "This Pussy Has Claws," "Chin Up, Fangs Out"—and to women's bodies—"Don't Tread on My Ovaries," "No Tampon Tax," and "Dear Congress, If you care so much about my vagina, Wash my period panties." There were signs emphasizing feminism—"Smash the Patriarchy," "Feminists Against Fascism," "Hear Us Roar,"—and men's support of women's rights—"Men Against Misogyny," "Men of Quality Don't Fear Equality." There were chants of "My body, my choice."

There was support for immigrant Americans: "My People Were Refugees Too," "Build Bridges, Not Walls," "Welcome, Immigrants, Thank You for Choosing America."

Many of the signs pointed specifically to Trump: "Left or Right, Trump is Wrong," "If You Aren't Angry, You Aren't Paying Attention," "We Are the Popular Vote," "Rise Against the Predator in Chief," "Protest is Patriotic," "Not My President," "Visualize Impeachment," "Putin's Pawn," "Inaugurate the Resistance," "Government is Not a Reality Show." One sign depicted Putin holding up an infant

Trump, with the words "Who's Your Daddy?" People chanted "Hey hey, ho ho, Donald Trump has got to go!" "We want a leader, not a creepy Tweeter!" and "This is what Democracy looks like!"

There were numerous variations on Hillary Clinton supporters' "I'm With Her" message; these now instead either pointed to images of the Statue of Liberty or were ringed with arrows pointing in all directions.

The mood was upbeat; while marchers wanted to make their grievances known, the experience of being in a vast crowd with shared purpose, rather than the small straggly rallies many had experienced before, gave the marchers a pervasive sense of joy and exhilaration. People began to smile, hug, dance; marchers waved to the police, who waved back. Neither Sam nor Jacobine, nor most of the marchers, could hear the speakers or see them on the Jumbotrons, but that didn't matter—they'd be able to hear later what had been said.

Gloria Steinem, one of a large roster of speakers, stated "Our constitution does not begin with 'I, the President.' It begins with, 'We, the People.' I am proud to be one of thousands who have come to Washington to make clear that we will keep working for a democracy in which we are linked as human beings, not ranked by race or gender or class or any other label."

So many people had come, of all ages and descriptions, that soon there was no actual march, just a gradual east-west flow of bodies, with many times and areas of stasis, of hundreds of people milling about enjoying each others' signs and costuming, climbing onto trees and equipment, photographing one another, lifting their hands and faces. Children danced, were lifted onto adults' shoulders.

Meanwhile, just after ten, Trump and family headed in the opposite direction of the march to attend the traditional National Prayer Service at the National Cathedral. Later, when he spoke at CIA headquarters in midafternoon, he stood in front of a wall carved with over a hundred stars commemorating the agents killed in the line of duty, and despite having recently likened the CIA to Nazis, told his audience that they were his "No. 1 stop" on his first full day in office, because they were "really special amazing people." Mostly, though, he boasted wildly about the attendance at his inauguration speech, and asserted that journalists who had debunked his claims were "among the most dishonest human beings on earth." He made no mention whatsoever of the Women's March that was still underway, where demonstrators were so visibly and overwhelmingly challenging him.

Late in the day, as marchers milled around the Ellipse within sight of the White House, they propped their signs against the wire fence that separated them from the White House lawn, then gradually they dispersed toward the Metro, which filled with masses of tired but exhilarated bodies.

At the end of the day, it was estimated that about 500,000 had participated in DC and perhaps two million nationally, to which could be added many in other countries in support. Jacobine's cousin Janie marched in Saskatoon, her friend in the Yucatán reported an event in Mérida, a friend in Prague spoke at the rally there, other friends went marching in Berlin and London; friends all over the US marched locally, and although Jacobine didn't catch sight of any familiar faces in DC, a great many of them subsequently posted photos on Facebook.

Meanwhile, Sean Spicer, Trump's first press secretary, held a press conference to claim that Trump's inauguration crowd "was the largest audience ever to witness an inauguration, period, both in person and around the globe," a claim which others immediately demonstrated to be wildly inaccurate. Trump's final campaign manager Kellyanne Conway then claimed Spicer's figures to be "alternative facts," which she was told were "falsehoods," perhaps because calling them lies was too straightforward to say on the national news. The dispute about the size of the inauguration crowd would continue for the remainder of the Trump presidency. Photographic evidence amply showed that the crowd had been far smaller than for the Obama inaugurations, and in fact a photograph distributed by the National Park Service was later revealed to have been doctored to make the Trump crowd look less pitiful.

Soon, estimates for the count at the Women's March rose to perhaps three million nationally, then later to something between three million and over five million, and over seven million worldwide. Certainly it had been the largest one-day protest in US history. But apart from righteous joy in such solidarity, Jacobine felt that the days since then had been pretty much a cascade of fascist horrors.

"Trump and his crowds have set forth on a rampage of destruction and lies," she commented to Beth after a faculty meeting. "It's a repeat of Nazi Germany, scapegoating the Muslims instead of the Jews. I listen to NPR, sign petitions, email my senators, etc. I'm up until midnight online."

"I know," said Beth. "I can't entirely tear myself away from the news even though I'd like to." Beth, who was up for tenure that year, seemed emotionally exhausted between stressors at school and the national news, and worried that despite a stellar record in all three of the required areas of teaching, research, and service, she might not get tenure.

Within days, Trump signed an executive order preventing nationals of seven majority-Muslim countries from entering the US—not, to be sure, the countries best known for producing terrorists, like Saudi Arabia—and immediately hundreds of people were stranded all over the world, some of them refugees, others simply US residents who had been visiting family abroad.

"Absolute chaos and panic," wrote Jacobine to a British friend. "Huge protests at major airports. A brave judge ruled against the order but people are still stranded." Indeed, as many as sixty thousand visas were "provisionally revoked."

Her cousin Sam remained afraid to do much, but did go out and photograph numerous protests, albeit without a sign of his own, working from the edges of the crowds to document the resistance.

Jacobine told Kerry, "Now that it's come out that the people arrested on felony charges on inauguration day aren't even thought to have been the ones who actually committed property damage, I can definitely see why Sam wants to be in a mobile position."

"Yes," said Kerry, "I've heard that journalists and bystanders were 'kettled' and unable to escape the police cordon. So wrong!"

Jacobine had the same kind of reaction as when, years before, her house had been broken into. Back then, she'd gone from room to room seething and vowing that the burglar had better not still be there. She now went to protests with peaceful intent but with an underlying readiness to attack anyone who attacked her. She told friends, "I value nonviolence, but if a Trump thug sets upon me at a protest, I expect to cause damage. Fortunately the anti-Trump contingent is large and vocal. We are not a tiny minority." Polls suggested that Trump's support among voters was lessening somewhat, although many who ought to have known better were still on his side.

"That crackpot Deb Dowd, who claims she's a liberal and who for some reason does have scads of anti-Trump Facebook friends, is still singing his praises," said Jacobine to another neighbor when they ran into one another at the farmer's market. "Get her going and she spews forth absolute gibberish, which may be why she likes Trump so much."

"I just don't understand her," said the neighbor. "She's very civic-minded in so many ways, but you're right about the gibberish."

"Yesterday," said Jacobine, "I posted about McCain and Graham's opposition to Trump—I thought that this would speak to the more conservative few among my Facebook people—and Deb responded with a bizarre comment about how she wouldn't have thought I'd voted for McCain/Palin and that it's time to get rid of the establishment so that's why people voted for Trump."

"Really!" said her neighbor.

"Yes—the woman knows next to nothing about me in any real sense and has only been even slightly acquainted with me for a few years, but now she's claiming I must've voted for McCain/Palin? What idiocy. As in, she knows that 1) I participate in neighborhood activities; 2) I'm a historian; 3) I don't support Trump. So yeah, she's a real expert on how I voted eight years ago."

Of course, it was counterproductive to be distracted by this dingbat Deb, someone Jacobine felt she should never have accepted as a Facebook "friend" since Jacobine had guessed from the start that Deb was bonkers. But people like Deb, she supposed, lapped up Kellyanne Conway's "alternative facts" and were too deranged to grasp that in a week the US had headed toward fascist dictatorship.

Indeed, Kellyanne Conway of the "alternative facts" promptly and illegally hawked Ivanka Trump's products on national TV, exhorting viewers, "Go buy Ivanka's stuff is what I would tell you. It's a wonderful line. I own some of it. I'm going to give a free commercial here: Go buy it today, everybody. You can find it online." Within hours, two organizations filed formal ethics complaints against Conway for violating the Hatch Act, which prohibited use of a federal position "for the endorsement of any product, service or enterprise." Public Citizen alleged that Conway's endorsement reflected "an on-going careless regard of the conflicts of interest laws and regulations" by "some members of the Trump family and Trump Administration," while Citizens for Responsibility and Ethics in Washington asserted that "This seems to us to be about as clear-cut a violation as you can find." Richard Painter, chief ethics attorney for George W. Bush, stated that "The events of the past week" demonstrated that neither the president, his family, nor the White House staff intended "to make meaningful distinctions between his official capacity as president and the Trump family business." But despite widespread condemnation of her behavior, Conway would continue to violate the Hatch Act, so that in June of 2019 the US Office of Special Counsel formally recommended that Conway be removed from federal service for her "egregious, notorious, and ongoing" violations, most of which by that time involved "disparaging Democratic presidential candidates while speaking in her official capacity during television interviews and on social media." Conway, however, protected by the president's peculiar notions of free speech, jeered "If you're trying to silence me through the Hatch Act, it's not going to work... Let me know when the jail sentence starts."

9

In early February, already exhausted by the ongoing madness of Trump's first days in Washington, Jacobine went down to Cinda's museum to hear a talk about one of the lesser-known French Impressionists, after which Cinda and Jacobine went out to one of their favorite haunts in that area, a cozy little restaurant that emphasized its vast selection of beers.

"I'm in this ongoing battle with the docents," said Cinda. "They have this idea that they should be in charge of educational programming, and that they know more than any of the employees whose job it actually is to devise the programming."

"What are they up to now?" asked Jacobine, for whom stories about the docents were a familiar staple of conversations with Cinda.

"There are some who are okay, of course, but most of them are just impossible. They imagine that because they taught second-grade math twenty years ago, or whatever, they must know all about museum education pedagogy. Well, they don't. First of all, they don't pay enough attention to the information we give them about the artworks, and we can't have them spouting incorrect information!"

"Well, no," said Jacobine, whose desire to have docents for her own museum invariably evaporated during conversations with Cinda.

"They don't seem to understand that they are volunteers, and that volunteers are supposed to work under staff supervision. The staff are professionals. We all have at least a master's degree in Art History or Museum Studies. We go to professional conferences to keep up in the field!"

"I know," said Jacobine, who as part of her job went to some of the same conferences.

"They keep fomenting little rebellions, where they claim 'But we've always done it this way!' or they refuse to prepare the activities that they're supposed to do with the school groups."

"Surely you can tell the worst ones that their services are no longer needed," said Jacobine. "After all, they're volunteers, so you don't even have to worry about presenting a watertight case for firing them the way you'd have to if they were employees."

"That's not how it works," said Cinda. "Besides, we can't claim we've got more docents than we need, because we don't have enough. And some of them like to go to Kyle and tittle-tattle about anything you say that they didn't like. It's a very weird little kindergarten-playgroundish world."

Cinda continued to recount further details about ways in which the docents had banded together to sabotage various programs that she and her colleagues had planned, and lamented that they claimed to be unavailable for trainings and public lectures such as the one Cinda and Jacobine had just attended.

It was a pleasant enough supper overall, but as was often the case, Jacobine grew tired of hearing about the museum docents' failings and their intransigence about programming, and about the general passivity and incompetence of the director of education. Cinda told these stories well enough, but Jacobine felt she had heard them quite a few times.

•   •   •

A week or so later, Cinda, Jacobine, and Kerry got together to attend a lecture at the university by the animal expert and autism advocate Temple Grandin, as Cinda was eager to hear whatever she might have to say about dog behavior, and Jacobine and Kerry had read her autobiography.

The crowd was enormous, filling much of the university's stadium, but the sound quality was not impressive, making it hard at times to make out just what Grandin was saying.

For the benefit of those in the audience who might not have read the story of her life, Grandin spoke about her childhood and struggle for education, and her work studying pigs and feedlot cattle. Much of what Grandin had to say, however, related to her efforts to understand how non-neurotypical people such as herself thought. She described herself as an associative thinker who thought in pictures, and she hypothesized that in addition to those like herself who thought in pictures—visual thinkers, she called them—there were others, who thought in patterns and could be called music and math thinkers; and finally, there were verbal logic thinkers. While Jacobine found this interesting, she was also skeptical of some of it. She herself often thought associatively, but not at all in pictures, and indeed she found Grandin's lecture a bit too associative and repetitive in its ideas for her taste. She was also not a fan of the trend to group people into "visual thinkers" and so on, which had permeated the country's college campuses in recent years and resulted in far too many of her students claiming that the reason they wrote poor history papers was that they were visual thinkers. Grandin's list of the types of thinkers and their traits was full of things that Jacobine did tolerably to well; she supposed that some people probably did fall strongly into one or another of the three categories, but whether *most* people did, or even most autism-spectrum people did, was another question. The slide Grandin showed of the three sets of traits did admit that one could have a mixture, but math was the only thing on any of the lists where Jacobine could be described as having a real deficit. She did not, however, imagine herself to be some sort of rare polymath whose only weakness was mathematics.

The question-and-answer period that followed Grandin's talk was long and at times emotional. An autistic youth seated near them wanted Grandin to know that video was very important to him and that he could not see why she wanted him to limit his screen-time. A young woman with Asperger's said that she was good at school but found other students distracting because they were so often silly. Another person with Asperger's called on everyone with a disability to raise their hands, which many did, whereupon he announced that everyone in the audience should have raised a hand because everyone was disabled in some way. There was much applause at this assertion.

"We are *not* all disabled," said Jacobine to her companions. "Everyone has weaknesses, but that doesn't make the entire population disabled. I'm not disabled just because I'm bad at math and have never been able to do a backbend." Whether Kerry and Cinda heard her amidst the thundering applause was unclear.

The questions continued, focusing almost entirely on disabilities, which while initially of interest to all three, eventually led them to leave the stadium.

Cinda was excited about the talk, saying "I've always wanted to hear her speak, she's done so much amazing work on behalf of animals."

"Yes, but so much of it relates to making them feel more comfortable about going to be slaughtered," said Kerry. "That always makes me feel a little weird."

"Me too," said Jacobine, "but on the other hand, if we're going to slaughter animals at all, I'd prefer that it be done as humanely as possible."

"But can we even call it humane to slaughter them?" said Kerry. "I mean, I do eat meat, so I participate in animal slaughter to some extent, but is it humane even if the animals aren't feeling stressed until the very last minute?"

"Less inhumane, then?" said Jacobine.

"I don't know," admitted Kerry.

There was a slight pause, and then Cinda exclaimed "I always *knew* I was just incapable of doing algebra!"

Jacobine sighed. "That seems implausible to me," she said. "Just because we didn't do well at high school algebra doesn't mean we're innately incapable of learning it."

"Oh, I'm quite sure that I'm incapable of learning it," said Cinda. She proceeded to tell a long story about how she had passed a required college math course because the professor felt sorry for her. "I could never have passed that course otherwise," she asserted.

During supper, Cinda updated them on her travails with the docents and her newish boss, as well as all about the recovery of one of her dogs from surgery and the latest on a recent job interview in Spokane, most of which

Jacobine had already heard when she had gone to dinner with Cinda after the museum talk the previous week.

Jacobine wished Kerry would say more to leaven the conversation. She felt she did not get much good conversation these days; yes, occasionally with this person or that, and her students were usually fun to talk with in a professor-student sort of way; but although there was not a shortage of intelligent, likeable people around, that was not the same as having genuinely good conversation. And one-on-one, while Cinda gave Jacobine time to answer her questions without interruptions, she neither made much effort to elicit anything from Jacobine nor made Jacobine feel like talking

10

That night Jacobine dreamt that pieces of a corpse were being loaded onto a bier, and then that she was becoming the corpse and starting to scream. She was pretty sure this was the only time she'd ever dreamt in such a classic nightmare manner that she'd woken up screaming.

The day continued to be off-kilter, and she concluded that she was apparently really *out of it*—she'd kept thinking it was Saturday, the day of the neighborhood chili cookoff, so she'd soaked a package of beans pointlessly early. And then she'd also imagined that her 1:15 doctor's appointment was at 2:00, so she nearly missed it. This kind of thing made Jacobine feel dreadfully senile, although it was true she'd always had this kind of absentminded forgetful tendency.

Once she arrived at the doctor's, the waiting room TV was going on and on about shingles and how important it was for elderly people to get vaccinated. Jacobine certainly didn't want to develop shingles, given how severely it had affected various members of her family. Her father, for instance, had declined rapidly after having shingles. And her aunts Edie and Betty had never fully recovered either—they had had nerve pain for the rest of their lives. But while Jacobine was at risk—she had had chicken pox as a child—was she old enough to get the new vaccine? She didn't really think so, as she'd heard it was recommended mainly for those over seventy.

Next came an ad for an anti-insomnia drug; its potential side effects sounded awful. And after that followed exhortations to exercise at least thirty minutes, at least five days a week. *Yeah right, that'd be nice*, grumbled Jacobine internally. *I walk to cafés to grade and I wander the neighborhood. That's about all I can manage beyond biking to the farmer's market on Saturdays. I feel like I spend my life in a cave working at school.*

Once in the exam room, her upper body wrapped in a flimsy disposable garment, there was the doctor to deal with.

"Hello Sunshine!" cried Dr. Fell as she bustled in. "How are you today? Smile! Why aren't you smiling? It's a beautiful day out!"

Jacobine could never bring herself to answer this oppressively cheerful mode of address, which invariably caused her to frown.

"Smiling is good for you!" exclaimed the doctor. "How are you doing?"

"Okay," said Jacobine grudgingly.

"What brings you here today, dear? Give me a nice big smile."

"It's my annual checkup. And I think I'm due for a tetanus shot." Jacobine had made a mental list of things she felt she should ask the doctor about, but this list had departed her mind immediately upon the doctor's entrance.

"Let me see, sweetheart. Yes, you are due for tetanus. We'll do that today before you go. Now it also looks like you are due for a colonoscopy. Overdue! Why have you not done your colonoscopy yet?"

Jacobine repressed a wrathful reply. "I had a colonoscopy exactly when I was supposed to. I don't know why you don't have it in your records. I went to the gastroenterologist that you referred me to, he did the procedure, and the results were completely normal. I don't know why you keep telling me that I haven't had a colonoscopy yet. It was one of the worst experiences of my life—I thought I was going to die of water poisoning during the prep."

"Now sweetheart, water toxicity is very rare. I'm sure you were not in any danger."

"I don't know why you think that. I nearly fainted and I projectile-vomited their horrible Gatorade mixture all over both the kitchen and bathroom floors. I could have been auditioning for *The Exorcist*."

"Well, so then you will not need another colonoscopy until you turn sixty, dear."

And so what she really needed was to find a new GP, one who didn't irritate her and didn't forget things. Jacobine had concluded that she just didn't do well with Dr. Fell; she found the woman condescending and infantilizing when she was probably merely trying to be pleasant. *We're just a poor match.*

11

Jacobine had errands to do near where Cinda lived, and it would be easy to drop by, so she arranged with Cinda to go over.

Cinda bustled about feeding the animals, picking up their toys, moving tools and paint cans, loading the dishwasher and washing some dishes by hand as she talked. Jacobine was used to seeing Cinda's living space in better order, but when she thought about it, she realized that it was Cinda's previous house that had always been in better order, whereas this one, although Cinda had lived there over a year, had never quite come together and always gave the impression that Cinda was still in the process of moving in. It was true, too, that Cinda's previous house had always seemed like a finished work of domestic art, beautifully and artistically arranged, a welcoming and comfortable space, whereas this house, which had had less character to begin with, seemed for the most part to resist Cinda's efforts to remodel and redesign it. This house retained a cramped, boxy layout in which every room felt a little too narrow, and the colors Cinda loved made it feel odd and dark rather than cozy and sophisticated as they'd been in the old house. The living room had a hard, low-budget feel to it despite Cinda's comfortable and ample couch and chairs, and despite her individual and well-chosen collection of paintings, prints, bowls, and small sculptures.

Cinda kept talking, but it was hard for Jacobine to focus on what she was saying; there was nothing much to focus on, for one thing. So much of what Cinda was saying consisted of "Can you hand me that..." and "When I get the cupboards in the kitchen refinished..." and "Marlow, would you stop spilling your water all over the floor?" The dogs kept moving restlessly, nervously, optimistically, back and forth through the kitchen, wagging their long tails and thrusting their noses at Cinda and Jacobine, barking from time to time, stretching to see whether there was anything of interest on the kitchen counters or in the dishwasher or in the trash, lying down suddenly on Cinda's or Jacobine's feet. Cinda made references to the dogs' health problems and which ones could eat which kinds of dog food or needed to be taken for weekly physical therapy; she talked about which vegetables Jacobine could chop for her and how difficult it was to find one of her favorite micro-brews in this part of the country; she reviewed options for selling her family's inherited property. It all made Jacobine want to leave. And somehow there was little real energy in the conversation, even from Cinda, so after supper Jacobine soon said she needed to get home and get a good night's sleep before work.

12

As February drew to a close, Jacobine attended another local anti-Trump rally. It was scheduled for Sunday at five o'clock, a bad time to gather any audience downtown, and she was disappointed to hear the speakers complain about the Democrats, which she considered unproductive and divisive. On the other hand, through the rally she did learn that "pink slip potluck parties" were being planned nationwide for the Ides of March, at which everyone would write postcards to the president and various members of Congress expressing dissatisfaction with their job performance.

She went to see *I Am Not Your Negro* at the nearby movie theater and then, at home, learned that the U.S. border control had harassed a seventy-year-old Australian children's author, who vowed never to return; while refugees already in the U.S. were reportedly tramping hours in the snow to the Canadian border to request asylum there. The City Council of Richmond, California, meanwhile, voted in support of impeaching Donald Trump, so Jacobine wrote them a thank-you letter.

13

In the late evening, Jacobine began to have strange chest pains. Influenced by her mother's repeatedly passing along articles on heart attacks, and by the recent death of her friend Fran's dear friend Miles, she betook herself to the hospital despite the fact that the last time mysterious chest pains had prompted her to go, the staff had demonstrated an alarming inability to bill her correctly.

Last time, in fact, they had fairly quickly decided that her chest pains were due to dehydration after forty miles on the regional bike trails with Cinda. This time they took her symptoms more seriously and kept her twenty hours for tests, so that in the morning she had to cancel class. She had brought along her cell phone but then couldn't find it to make the call; the nurse told her it hadn't been found in the hospital and that no, she couldn't go out to look for it in her car. Later, after she was discharged, it turned out that she really *had* dropped it at the hospital, because the Lost and Found department had messaged Kerry in the middle of the night, whereupon Kerry had called Jacobine's phone to find out what was going on, only to have the person who answered deny that Jacobine was a patient at the hospital. So there had been misinformation all around about the phone, but she was finally able to retrieve it.

And meanwhile, the hours of tests showed no sign of heart trouble. That was encouraging, except that Miles's doctors hadn't found anything wrong with his heart either and then it had killed him a week later.

14

Cinda called and began talking about her current plans to enjoy the great outdoors, but because she refused to have a land line and her house was not well designed for cell phone reception, the call kept breaking up and being dropped.

"I'm seriously thinking about getting a trailer RV for camping," she declared during a period of comprehensibility. This wasn't a new plan; she had been talking about this for at least the past year, but funds and logistics had always been a problem. "I'd need to get a different car in order to be able to tow the model of trailer I'm hoping to get," she said. "The car I have now just won't haul it. Which is too bad, because I like my car. It handles well and it has a good amount of space for the dogs as well as for luggage." Cinda began to detail the technical requirements for towing the trailer of her choice, which caused Jacobine to respond with iterations of "Uh huh" and "Wow."

"I might be able to get the trailer I want used for about $14,000, but there aren't any for sale locally," said Cinda. "The nearest one I've been able to find is in Kentucky."

"Well, that's not an impossible distance," observed Jacobine. "You could always rent a suitable truck to go bring it home."

"That's a thought," admitted Cinda. "In fact, I could rent something to tow it whenever I wanted to go camping, and then I wouldn't have to buy a new car."

Unbidden, the image of Lucille Ball in the movie *The Long, Long Trailer* leaped into Jacobine's mind. She attempted to banish the thought of objects rolling wildly about as the trailer climbed mountain roads...

"My siblings and I will probably sell our parents' riverfront property this year," said Cinda, "in which case I'd have some disposable income. One of the neighbors wants to buy it, but he's not offering market value." Cinda expanded on this problem at length, then said "My brother Gordon might buy the property from the rest of us, which I think would be a much better solution." Cinda had a great deal to say about why this would be better than selling to the neighbor, which made Jacobine begin to feel a bit tired.

"Meanwhile there's a lot of traveling I want to do," continued Cinda. "I just need to come up with travel partners for some of it. So one of the things I want to do in the near future is this coast-to-coast hike."

"Coast to coast? Hiking? Do you have any idea how long that would take?"

"Well, I don't know exactly, but it's very manageable."

"Coast to coast? Manageable? On foot?" Jacobine could not believe what she was hearing.

"England isn't all that wide," said Cinda. "I'm sure a person could do it in under two weeks."

"England?"

"I've had this on my bucket list for a long time, hike across England, do a walking tour from one coast to the other."

"Okay, then I guess that sounds doable," said Jacobine, who was aware that the British had a venerable tradition of walking the land.

"Of course it is. We'll need to figure out the transport, though," said Cinda.

"What do you mean, the transport?" Jacobine had no idea what Cinda was talking about. If you were going to England from North America, obviously you flew. The age of ocean-liners had long since passed.

"Well, who is going to drive our gear to the next inn for us while we walk?"

"I don't get what you're talking about. Why would you need anything driven for you? You're on a walking tour, aren't you?"

"I don't know about you, but I don't want to carry all that stuff day after day," said Cinda. "Now, on the one hand we could join a group that will handle all those logistics and have everyone's gear driven each day, but I don't really want to go with a group."

Jacobine said, "Walking across England and staying at inns is not exactly back-country camping with a huge backpack. You could certainly do it with a smaller backpack in the summer—some changes of clothes, some toiletries, your iPhone, a thick sweater, a rain poncho, some maps. Voilà. You're not talking about climbing Mount Everest with native bearers and Sherpas."

Cinda said, "I don't want to lug any of that along the way." She continued, "So, when do you want to go? I'd much rather the two of us just went by ourselves, except that I don't want to have to do all the planning involved in figuring out how many miles we'll walk each day and where to lodge and how to move the gear from place to place."

Jacobine said, "I'm sure you'd enjoy walking across England, but this isn't something I see myself doing. I have a lot of other things that are higher priorities for my summers. You know that's the only time I can do my immigration research abroad."

"You'd be the perfect travel companion, though!" said Cinda.

"Sorry, you'll have to get someone else," said Jacobine. "This is not something I can do."

"But you have relatives in the British Isles," said Cinda.

"Walking coast to coast in England isn't a way for me to hang out with my third cousins who live in Glasgow. You'll just have to find someone else, or go with one of those groups."

15

Despite a good start to her class on The Immigrant Experience 1840–1920, and despite life generally proceeding smoothly enough, Jacobine now often had the disturbing feeling that she was not going to live much longer. There were times when she suspected that one day she'd learn she had an incurable disease—pancreatic cancer, for instance—and needed to plan better what was to become of her files and such; and then there were times when it was less her own personal extinction that seemed nigh and rather that climate change would soon wipe out humankind entirely so that all she'd striven for or cared about would be of no consequence.

It wasn't that she was continually afflicted with these thoughts, but both scenarios were entirely possible. To be sure, she'd eventually die no matter what, and humans would eventually become extinct, but it wasn't distressing to envision herself living to ninety and the species lasting another thousand or more years. It was the thought of imminent extinction that disturbed her.

Meanwhile, Kerry was distracted and frazzled; her elderly cousin, who lived not too far away and was one of the relatives Kerry often visited, was declining rapidly. And then Kerry's cousin died, leaving Kerry as executor. It appeared that Cinda and Jacobine would not be seeing much of her for a while as she struggled with the complexities of an insufficiently well-organized estate.

And events in Washington were continuing to be wild. In January, the House and Senate intelligence committees had launched parallel investigations into possible Russian interference in the election. In February, Trump's first national security adviser, Michael Flynn, had resigned after it came out that he had misled the FBI and the Vice President about the nature and content of his communications with the Russian ambassador. But Representative Nunes, who had been part of the Trump transition team and who chaired the House intelligence committee, quickly denied that the intelligence community had actual evidence of contact between the Trump campaign and Russian operatives. Rejecting numerous calls for an investigation by a select committee, he claimed the House should not engage in a "witch hunt." Nunes then announced that he wouldn't seek to investigate Flynn's ties to Russia, because Flynn had been "doing this country a favor" and "should be thanked for it." In Jacobine's view, to be sure, Nunes was a Trump lackey sabotaging the investigation that he was supposedly chairing.

Meanwhile, the FBI too was investigating Russian ties to the Trump campaign and administration; Congress was voting on a so-called replacement for the Affordable Care Act; and the country was awaiting confirmation of Neil Gorsuch to the Supreme Court. Gorsuch's confirmation might have been uncontroversial, had it not been for the fact that President Obama's choice for the vacancy, Merrick Garland, had not been confirmed due to the unprecedented refusal of the Republican-held Senate to hold a hearing or vote, on the grounds that the next president should fill the vacancy instead. This tactic had resulted in the expiration of Garland's nomination in January of 2017 and cries that Garland's rightful seat on the bench had been stolen.

During all of this Trump, as was typical of him, kept providing circular distractions, prompting the South African comedian Trevor Noah to describe him as a magician who never finishes a trick but just keeps starting new ones. Trump and his administration were proving ideal fodder for satire...

But Washington was not the only site of worrisome developments. On March 22nd a British man drove a rented vehicle into pedestrians on the pavement along London's Westminster Bridge, injuring more than fifty people and killing several. After crashing the car into the palace grounds fence, he ran into New Palace Yard, where he fatally stabbed a police officer in his attempt to reach Parliament, whereupon he was shot dead by another officer. The attacker had converted to Islam in prison and claimed to be waging jihad in revenge for Western military action in the Middle East; presumably his mode of attack had been inspired by the previous year's Bastille Day truck attack in Nice, where a Tunisian resident of France had killed 86 and injured 458.

Without even waiting for the Westminster attack to end, Trump Junior tweeted, insulting the Muslim mayor of London for having said, months earlier, that being prepared for terrorism was part of living in a great global city. Unabashed by British and indeed global disgust at his insensitivity at a time of shock and mourning, Junior would continue to insult London's mayor in the coming years. Trump Senior, of course, kept insulting American allies more generally and proffering praise of Putin.

Posters now began to appear in local cafés, announcing "Hate has no home here"; much good was visible locally but none of this deterred the Trump administration, which along with its political follies and human rights violations was not merely denying the existence of climate change but was actively exacerbating global warming and the impending extinction of countless species.

16

After the Westminster attack, Jacobine awoke from a dream in which she had died and was being pumped full of an embalming fluid. This fluid then had the curious result of partly reviving the dead person—Jacobine—to climb out of the coffin in search of a bathroom in order to expel the excess fluid; yet all the same, she knew she would need to have another round of embalming fluid in order to die fully.

Once awake from this unpleasant dream, she lay in bed awhile, pondering reports that as the Arctic ice melted, the planet could potentially experience a lethal methane burp at any time, an event that would result in mass extinction.

How she hated this feeling of winding down toward death in a country moving toward fascism and ecological collapse! Surely she was too young to feel death racing towards her; most of the time she was immersed in life, after all. Yet the feeling gnawed at her, making her wonder all too frequently whether she had some undetected fatal ailment. You didn't have to be old to die. After all, just among people she knew well, her friend Leo had died of an aneurysm, Doron had died of throat cancer, Morgan's liver cancer had ultimately got him, Fran had terminal lung cancer, and Tom Ward had just announced the death of his brother.

17

Although Jacobine's friend Fran had been diagnosed with lung cancer over a year ago, it had been Jacobine's understanding that the prognosis was good for Fran to live a fairly normal life for several more years. Jacobine hadn't spoken to Fran, who lived in Berkeley, in several months—they had last spoken when Fran's friend Miles, an acquaintance of Jacobine's, had died so unexpectedly—but although Fran found her chemotherapy painful and exhausting, in between the chemo treatments she had reported that she had time to regain her strength and go for gentle walks, see friends, and even go on short trips. Now, however, Jacobine learned that the situation had changed.

> Tamsin Gold tamsing@gmail.com
> Mar 31, 2017, 1:39 AM
> to Jacobine, Lili Ann, Marina
>
> Fran appears to be ending her journey. She is very frail and probably does not have much longer to live. She's at Alta Bates hospital. She's surrounded by all her family... including the extended one... if you were here that obviously would include you. I saw her earlier this week and told her how much I love her. Tonight I went to the hospital. Mostly she

slept. But when she awoke, I walked in. She was surrounded by friends. Her eyes were mostly closed (she's on morphine) but she smiled and even laughed. She kept saying how lucky she was to be surrounded by all that love. I think everyone in the room felt the same way: we were the lucky ones. Lucky and honored to be able to be there for the end of this magnificent journey.

I'm overwhelmed. I know you would want to know, and of course, you would want to be there by her side. I am going back tomorrow and I will tell Fran how much you love her. Because I know you do.

Who knows? Maybe Fran will rally, but the doctors aren't optimistic. So I'm sending love.

Tamsin

Jacobine Flaa Flaa.di.dah@gmail.com
Mar 31, 2017, 10:24 AM
to Tamsin, Lili Ann, Marina

This is such sad news to wake up to!

Like Tamsin, I'm overwhelmed with feelings. For me, there's a lot of No, No, not yet!! Not already! We all feel that, of course, but for me it's intensified by sadness that I have not seen Fran since her diagnosis. So there is guilt too. A few months ago, Fran was still taking long walks and having pretty good spells between treatments. However, not getting a Christmas card was a sign things were going downhill as Fran was so good about sending cards.

Fran has always created a magic around her of warmth and compassion, and yes, gently encouraging us all to be better people and to follow our best dreams. She always had wisdom and a sense of humor about our lives and life's journey. She was endlessly hospitable too, as we all know!

It makes me very sad that if she goes in the next few days, I will not have seen her again and told her in person how much she means to me.

Missing you all, but especially Fran!

Love, Jacobine

Lili Ann Wold perchance@yahoo.com
Mar 31, 2017, 3:22 PM
to Jacobine, Tamsin, Marina
Hello all,

This is such sad news. I'll be in the Bay Area next week and was so hoping to see Fran again! I did get to see her last June and am so happy about that. Though we know that death awaits us all, it's so painful when it actually arrives.

Fran was a stellar human being. Please tell her how much I have loved her. It was an honor to be her friend, and I can't picture the world without her. Am so glad she's surrounded by family and friends. Am sending my love too to support her in her transition.

A big hug to all,

Lili Ann

Marina Marston m&mgal@gmail.com
Mar 31, 2017, 6:49 PM
to Jacobine, Lili Ann, Tamsin

Someday I hope we can all be together for a day and have our own celebration of Fran's life. The beautiful coming-together of people around her right now is a testament to how she lived her life.

I'm feeling paralyzed. I can't do anything much except take walks, even though I have tons of work.

Jacobine Flaa Flaa.di.dah@gmail.com
Mar 31, 2017, 6:52 PM
to Marina, Tamsin, Lili Ann

I have to walk too. This is so hard.

Jacobine picked up her camera and left the house, walking fast. Usually when out for a walk with her camera, she walked slowly, moving into an attentive state in which she noticed things that otherwise eluded her—interesting shadows or sidewalk cracks, graffiti, patches of peeling paint, broken sculptures, ruins, industrial machinery— but today the camera was more of a prop, an object that might at some point later in her walk prove useful, but was not at present a means of seeing in new ways. The spring evening was warm, the air fresh, the sun becoming lower in the sky. And so Jacobine walked and walked, walking for miles, walking till dark and a little after that, with fast firm steps but pausing frequently, pausing in pain, pausing to wipe her eyes.

Upon her return, there was a new email.

> Tamsin Gold tamsing@gmail.com
> Mar 31, 2017, 9:38 PM
> to Jacobine, Marina, Lili Ann
>
> I just left the hospital. Fran is going into in-hospital hospice care today. They think she'll go at any moment. I was there for several hours and she was sleeping the whole time. She's on morphine and oxygen. They removed the feeding tube because it was irritating. They say that people who are dying can still hear, so I talk to her. I told her how much each one of you love her. I got the feeling she was understanding, but her lucid moments seem few and far between. Even if you could be there it would simply be in support. I feel very lucky I could be there. I'm not sure I'm going to be able to go back. I think if Fran could, she'd tell you that it's OK and she loves you. Yes let's get together. Let's find a way.

Fran had been such a support to so many over the years—supporting friends through broken romances, through difficult job searches, through creative and scholarly projects. Jacobine was sure that Fran knew to some extent that friends were thinking of her and sending love, but she was also aware that often people don't realize or accept how much others actually care about them. She knew that people so often feel insecure about the love that others feel for them, and so often don't realize the extent to which they may have made a difference in others' lives. Knowing this, Jacobine couldn't feel as sure as she'd have liked that Fran truly knew how much her distant friends missed her and grieved in advance for her loss.

· ·

The next morning, Jacobine awoke to waves of sadness. She didn't even know whether Fran was still alive at that moment. Tamsin had been good about sending updates, but she could hardly camp out at the hospital every day. Jacobine thought, *The more I think over what Fran gave us, the more astounded and grateful I am. I don't usually think in terms of wanting or needing a role model, but I realize that in many ways Fran has been one for me in her phenomenal generosity of spirit.*

Jacobine called her mother, who had left a message the day before. She suspected her mother was sensing something was wrong, as her mother sometimes had a surprising ability to pick up on her times of sadness. This time, however, her mother assumed that Jacobine must be under a lot of stress at work, which was not really the case.

"There's some stuff happening at work, of course, but it doesn't usually affect my mood all that much," said Jacobine. "No, right now the main thing that's going on is that my friend Fran is dying."

Jacobine's mother had met Fran a fair number of times over the years when they had all lived in California, but she now claimed to have no recollection of Fran. "My memory isn't what it used to be," she asserted. It was true that her memory wasn't as good as it had once been, but even so it was hardly poor. "How long have you known Fran?" she asked.

"Close to thirty years."

Jacobine's mother conceded that that was a long time. She was sympathetic in a generic sort of way but apparently just could not recall that over the years she'd had entire conversations with Fran.

"I used to spend New Year's at Fran's fairly regularly," said Jacobine. "I always saw her when I went back to California."

"I'm afraid I just don't remember."

It was a reminder that not only was Jacobine's mother nearly ninety, but that she had really never been very interested in retaining any awareness of almost any of Jacobine's friends. True, she didn't know most of them, but she had once known about Fran, just hadn't bothered to retain the knowledge. In this respect her mental makeup, so focused on the present despite an interest in history, was simply alien to Jacobine. But there was nothing to be done about it. She would remember certain people—Jacobine could think of about five friends whom her mother was likely to recall—but if Fran hadn't made that list, then surely very few indeed of Jacobine's friends remained in her mind.

The conversation was mildly dispiriting on top of Jacobine's awareness of Fran's imminent demise. It meant that Jacobine had relatively few people with whom to share her impending loss, as while both women had many friends, they hadn't happened to have all that many in common—mainly Tamsin, Marina, and Lili Ann, although Jacobine had introduced a few others to Fran over the years.

• • •

Fran died early the next morning.

Tamsin Gold tamsing@gmail.com
Sun, Apr 2, 2017, 9:06 AM
to Lili Ann, Jacobine, Marina

Fran passed away peacefully at 4:15 AM.
When the nurses came to check, she had
gone. Janie told me she dreamt that they were
taking the oxygen off and she had one last
chance to talk to her mother, so she asked if
Fran had anything to tell her. And Fran told
her to thank everyone who came. That's so
Fran.

When I left last night, I had a very strong
feeling that she would go soon. I felt that Fran
was waiting for everyone to leave and for
Bernie to fall asleep. She couldn't leave a
party until she was the last one :-)

It was a good death. And a remarkable life.
Thanks for being there with me, because I felt
you were.

Love,

Tamsin

Lili Ann Wold perchance@yahoo.com
Sun, Apr 2, 2017, 9:27 AM
to Tamsin, Jacobine, Marina

Thanks so much for the news. I feel so sad to lose her. She was such a shining light.

Love to all,

Lili Ann

Jacobine Flaa Flaa.di.dah@gmail.com
Sun, Apr 2, 2017, 9:28 AM
to Tamsin, Lili Ann, Marina

I'm so glad the end was peaceful and that you felt we were there with you for Fran.

The last few days have made me think a lot about how much Fran meant to me. This is a very difficult transition, and what I am feeling can only be a fraction of what her family and those closest to Fran are experiencing.

Love to all,

Jacobine

Tamsin Gold tamsing@gmail.com
Sun, Apr 2, 2017, 9:32 AM
to Jacobine, Lili Ann, Marina

I think being there actually made it easier. It was an honor. I'm sorry you couldn't be there in body but I really felt you were there. You made it so much better for me. I felt so supported. I hope you also felt support. What an amazing community she created.

Jacobine Flaa Flaa.di.dah@gmail.com
Sun, Apr 2, 2017, 9:56 AM
to Tamsin, Lili Ann, Marina

Fran was such a remarkable person. I don't recall realizing that back when I first knew her (although of course I liked her), but in the—what, 29?—years of our friendship, she blossomed into a person who became her best self insofar as was possible in the time she had, shining the way for all who knew her.

Marina Marston m&mgal@gmail.com
Sun, Apr 2, 2017, 11:51 AM
to Jacobine, Lili Ann, Tamsin

You're right. She became her best self.

Fran's death was hard to grapple with. Jacobine managed to teach the day's class with composure, but when she met briefly with one of her students who was struggling emotionally, it became very hard to maintain a calm demeanor.

"I lost an old friend this morning," she said. "But I guess I hope to learn from Fran's example and be a better friend and teacher, and someone whom others want to be like."

Lexi being Lexi and in worship of all of her professors, they being her most genuine parents, said Jacobine was very strong and she hoped to be like her someday. And Jacobine knew that, whatever her own weaknesses and imperfections, she was already an inspiration to Lexi.

18

The morning of April 4th began with news of numerous deaths and hundreds of injured from a gas attack in Khan Sheikhoun, a rebel-held town in Syria's Idlib province— the victims were mostly children, it seemed, just horrible. Doctors reported that people were vomiting and foaming at the mouth, while others lost consciousness and suffered muscle spasms. Sarin or a related poison was suspected; in fact, it was possible that more than one type of gas had been released. The Syrian military denied using any toxic or chemical agents, but as the UN had already found the Syrian army guilty of using chemical weapons on three other occasions, it was generally suspected that this was a related attack on the civilian population.

Next came confirmation that the previous day's explosion in the St. Petersburg Metro, which had killed at least eleven people, had been the result of a bomb rather than an accident—a second, undetonated, bomb had been found. Asked about the attacks, Donald Trump said, vaguely, "Happening all over the world, absolutely a terrible thing."

Fran's death at least hadn't been caused by another human being.

19

In the days after Fran's death, Jacobine recognized that of late, even before learning that Fran was about to die, she'd been unusually labile, more sensitive than usual to any emotional stimulus, more open and less private or reserved than was typical of her during this period of her life. She now wept frequently about Fran, but also in response to reports of melting glaciers, the loss of permafrost, the deaths of lions, rhinos, gorillas, whales, vaquitas, and honeybees.

At the local pub, where Jacobine had gone to get away from home and grief, it began to storm—huge masses of water flooding out of the sky, whipped by wind so that the patterns of the gusts were visible on the wet pavement. A fierce hailstorm was hitting now, battering the roof, making the pavement white. A white river was rushing down the storm drain by the marked bike lane, looking foamy with hail. Nothing further than the other side of the street was clearly visible anymore. More water was rushing along the street, and faster, than the drain could swallow. Then, finally, the hail began to let up. Occasional lightning flashed. Cars passed at normal speeds now, scattering the hail, although around the corner Harold Street looked like an Arctic ice floe.

Then it was just rain; the barmaid wiped leaks from the window and went out to sweep the hail from the sidewalk; the street's hail had already mostly melted. That which remained was like pearls but less lustrous, more like rock salt.

On Jacobine's way home the sidewalk was covered with new green leaves cut by the hail.

•   •   •

On April 6th, Representative Nunes temporarily stepped aside from leading the House Russia investigation while the Office of Congressional Ethics investigated allegations, which he denied, that he'd improperly disclosed classified information to the public. Since this related to the Trump campaign, Nunes was criticized for giving the administration information on the investigation without also providing it to Adam Schiff, his Democratic counterpart on the Intelligence Committee.

20

At home on a quiet Sunday afternoon, Jacobine sat working in one of her upstairs rooms, one of the only places in the house to receive significant natural light, due to the fact that she had installed skylights shortly after moving in. It was a cheerful, lively-looking room, which she had painted a fresh green and decorated with house plants, an Amish quilt, and Mexican ceramics. White IKEA cube units stored boxes of stuff, and all around were bursts of strong color. This room, at this moment, appeared to her as an antidote to the stress created by Fran's death, the looming climate disaster, the Syrian refugee crisis, the recurrent school shootings that had become a norm in life in the US, and the unpredictable shocks and craziness of the Trump administration, in which appointees were specifically chosen for their incompetence or hatred of whatever they were to oversee, and where any regulation to protect human health or the natural environment was rapidly being scrapped.

Yet while she was fond of her house, Jacobine nevertheless supposed that in retirement she would probably like to live somewhere else, certainly somewhere with more natural light, perhaps a one-story for safety as she aged. While her living situation was pleasant enough, and she had many acquaintances, she felt genuinely close to almost no one in the area, nor were there that many people with whom she just *did* things—Cinda being one of the most reliably available prospects for biking, ice skating, concert-going, and dining. Prior to graduate school, Jacobine had spent her adult life in Northern California, so that despite her Midwestern roots, she didn't feel truly at home with Midwestern modes of socializing, which seemed to be so marital and neighborhood-based. She knew that there were interesting people in the area, she just didn't end up very well acquainted with very many of them. She supposed she wasn't all that good at meeting people—when she was younger, it had simply happened without much effort, and now it didn't. Maybe this was just a result of her being older now and liking to stay home and read.

And if only her mother hadn't felt obliged to sell the last house their family had owned in California! Despite the financial profit, what a loss the sale represented! It was not that it had been unreasonable for her elderly mother to sell the house in order to move into an apartment near her mother's younger sister Rose, but to sell a modest, charming, convenient house, the likes of which Jacobine would never herself be able to afford to buy there unless climate change destroyed California's economy during her lifetime! It had had light, a garden, was good for parties, was near BART and a bike path, and there was good freeway access—well, what was done was done.

21

Tax time arrived, and a nationwide Tax March was announced to protest Trump's failure to release his tax returns as was normal for the president to do. Emails began to fly urging attendance.

> "Jacobine, during the presidential campaign, Donald Trump became the first major nominee to refuse to release his tax returns in 40 years. We won't stop until we get the full transparency we deserve from the highest office in the land. He works for us now. Join thousands of Americans ALL ACROSS THE COUNTRY marching on April 15th!"

Oregon's Senator Wyden emailed too, saying:

> "We need to know: Is Trump fighting for working families or defending billionaires and special corporate interests? Let's raise our voices and be so loud that Trump cannot ignore us any longer. Once we know the truth about Trump's taxes we can keep fighting for a more fair tax system that works for everyone, not just the wealthy few. Get your friends to RSVP to join you at the Tax March on Saturday."

So Jacobine again made herself a sign and walked downtown to join in. The local Tax March was not among the larger ones in the nation, but all the same there was a decent turnout—although mainly people older than Jacobine, retirees. Everyone listened politely to the speakers, clapped, waved their signs. She supposed most people went to the larger rally at the Capitol, but all the same, it was important to hold these smaller local rallies too.

22

Around this time Jacobine began to wonder whether she had developed a vaginal infection; her labia were tending to feel sore, as if chafed. In general, she associated vaginal infections with sex—or at least that was generally how she had gotten them in the past—but she hadn't been having sex, so she supposed that the hormonal changes of menopause could have thrown off the pH balance, or that the normal microbial balance had been disrupted by poor sleep or by bike riding or who knew what. She did use a hormonal cream that her gynecologist had recommended the previous year, when riding her bike had become seriously uncomfortable and she had discovered that her labia looked shockingly thin and withered, but maybe the cream wasn't doing its job. Certainly her genitalia, when examined in the mirror, still did not look anything like their plump former selves.

So Jacobine went to the gynecologist, who said everything looked better than it had the year before and that she saw no sign of infection. "You can continue the hormonal cream, but you can also apply some externally, and that might resolve the intermittent soreness you've been experiencing."

"What if I actually happen to have sex?" asked Jacobine. She didn't know whether she would ever have sex again, but it was certainly possible, and she didn't think most men were likely to want to get a dose of estrogen during intercourse.

"Well, so long as you apply the cream after sex rather than before, the cream shouldn't be a problem for your partner," said the gynecologist, "and even if it does get onto a man's skin, it's not anything to worry about."

"That's fortunate," said Jacobine. She felt it would be even more fortunate if she were to have sex again before she died.

But although the exam was brief and not really unpleasant, at home that afternoon Jacobine realized that she felt like crawling into bed and napping. Perhaps it was because the spring weather had turned chilly. Or perhaps she was just ready for a rest after some nights during which she had not always slept well. In any event, next thing she knew, she had slept all afternoon, and by nine o'clock she felt ready to crawl right back into bed.

Jacobine could feel herself getting older, less flexible. She knew she still looked surprisingly young, but when parts of her body were atrophying—important parts, for heaven's sake—there was no point in pretending it wasn't happening. One of these days she'd look in the mirror and see that she looked older than dirt. Worse than looking older than dirt, one of these days she'd *feel* older than dirt.

She felt slightly trapped. She had interesting projects both at the museum and at home and she enjoyed working on them, but when not in the midst of something, she often felt moody and mildly depressed. Since she had mostly worked low-paid jobs in the nonprofit sector before getting her PhD and being hired at the university, she didn't see how she could retire early. She'd need to stay in her job until she was at least sixty-five. Of course, that was still some years in the future, but not all that many— sixty-five would arrive in a hurry because time was already racing by for her as it was, and anyway, she'd been born too late for the traditional sixty-five to be her Social Security retirement date, let alone a good time to begin collecting her small pension. Had she been financially independent, she could have picked and chosen exactly what she wanted to work on—been an independent scholar and curator, perhaps—but as it was, she was frequently distracted by administrative tasks, teaching-related tasks, and committee tasks, which made her weary.

Before turning in for the night, she took a quick look at Facebook, and saw a post from a pal from her college days.

"I started getting notices from the AARP when I was 50," said Doug. "I joined briefly (there ARE some good discounts) and then let my membership lapse. Recently re-joined and I've noticed something. When I first joined, probably about 50–60% of each e-newsletter I'd get was about vacations and retirement, with the rest being mainly about health. Now about 50-60% is about what's new in the work place, with 20-30% about health and maybe 10% about being retired and vacationing.

"Yeah, 'retired' now means 'still working.' America!"

This post, not surprisingly, was getting a lot of comment. Some people noted that studies had shown how important it was to continue to have interests in life and that retirement could be bad for the health. Others, however, pointed out that they weren't lacking in interests and looked forward to having more time to pursue them in retirement, assuming they weren't flat broke when retirement arrived.

Jacobine typed "Can I please stop having to grade papers and exams and just spend my days thinking up cool exhibitions about Ellis Island, homesteading, and how women got the vote?"

She closed the laptop, turned off the light, and fell asleep.

23

Mary Green <MLGreen62@gmail.com>
Thu, Apr 20, 2017, 1:33 PM
to Neighborhood

This may be the hardest message I've ever had to write. Greg Stevenson has passed away after a heart attack. Wednesday evening he was complaining of chest pains and his wife Laurie drove him to the hospital. However, his symptoms intensified and things went downhill fast. He didn't make it.

Yes, it's true. No, I can't believe it, either.

Greg moved here in the early 1990s. He is a past president, has served as Housing Liaison, and was in the process of creating the Block Captains committee. He always worked hard to make this community a better place. Just about everybody liked Greg, and Greg liked just about everybody in return. We have lost not only one of the best neighbors you could ever hope to have, but also a true friend.

Visitation and services will be Monday evening at Doane Funeral Home on Stafford Avenue. I will forward full info later today.

Laurie is not up for visitors right now. If you would like to reach out to her, please drop her an email or send a card. If you'd like to leave her a gift or a casserole, put it on her porch.

With the saddest of hearts, Mary Green

Two days later, out of nowhere, Jacobine began to feel sad, overflowing with emotion as she had when Fran was dying, so she supposed that Fran's death, combined with Greg Stevenson's unexpected death from a heart attack, was prompting this intense sadness. She couldn't bear to sit at home, so she went for a two-hour evening walk along the river. The weather was mild, the setting sun golden, the light upon the river so sparkling as sun gave way to reflections of lamplight, but all the same...

The walk helped some—she still felt sad but the feeling was no longer quite so overwhelming. Upon returning home, it occurred to her that she hadn't checked the mail in a day or two.

There was a card-sized envelope with an unfamiliar Sacramento address. As a former Californian, Jacobine knew a few people who lived in Sacramento, but she hadn't thought any of them had her postal address. With some trepidation, she opened the envelope and learned that Marjorie Fanning, a family friend, had died of leukemia.

Marjorie had written a note to include in the announcement sent by her children, Jacobine's old playmates. Jacobine thought, *My mother must be regretting she didn't take up any of Marjorie's invitations to travel together or at least visit.* The two had been good friends, although Jacobine supposed the friendship might have meant less to her mother than to the more extroverted Marjorie. Then again, it might have meant more to her mother precisely because she was more reserved. Such things were hard to judge, as Marjorie had more friends overall, but nonetheless valued Jacobine's family highly, whereas Jacobine's mother was usually content with writing the occasional letter to her three or four old friends, yet did also enjoy seeing them now and then.

Jacobine thought, *This must be why I felt so awful—this and Fran and Greg.* She now noticed that the answering machine light was blinking, and discovered that her mother had left a message about Marjorie's death.

Jacobine called her mother, who said "I thought I should call to let you know about Marjorie." Jacobine's mother had received the news the day before, which was perhaps when the announcement had arrived in Jacobine's mailbox as well.

Jacobine thought her mother sounded cheerful enough now, but that didn't mean she hadn't been grieving intensely two hours earlier when Jacobine had suddenly begun to feel so sad; it had been Jacobine's experience that sometimes she felt unexpectedly down when, unbeknownst to her, her mother was in a rare mood of grief or frustration. This had happened every so often after the death of Jacobine's father, when her mother and thousands of others in California's PERS system had suddenly lost their health insurance during a poorly managed computer upgrade, and also when various stock certificates accidentally left out of her parents' family trust had had to be properly reissued. One might be able to handle one's grief at losing a beloved but rapidly declining spouse after sixty years of marriage, but nonetheless be quite overwhelmed at learning that years of meticulous planning hadn't succeeded in making it easy to settle the estate.

Jacobine noted that her mother didn't exactly stay on topic during the call—rather than talking about Marjorie, Jacobine's mother wanted to talk about what a good thing it was that Jacobine had recently found someone to help her with yard work. Jacobine's mother seemed almost fixated on this, which caused Jacobine to wonder whether this was just standard maternal solicitousness or if there was something else involved. Having help with yard work did not loom large in Jacobine's mind.

Jacobine herself was unequivocally upset that Marjorie Fanning had died. As with Marjorie's husband Rowland, who had died a few years earlier, the loss of Marjorie meant that an important link to her childhood and much else had vanished. Marjorie's note, however, was a solace. "I live in your memories," Marjorie had written. This was something Jacobine believed: that whether or not human souls continued in any form (if indeed the soul existed to begin with), one survived in the memories of those one knew. This gave some people a long and strong afterlife and others very little, but so be it. Those with children or younger friends or who accomplished something survived in this manner for a time.

These were things Jacobine would have discussed with Fran, whether in person, by phone, or via email. There remained other possible people with whom such conversations could occur, but she felt as though there was no one anymore whom she'd actually call and talk through it with, especially anyone in the area where she now lived. She supposed Kerry would be there for her if called upon—they had talked about Jacobine losing Fran, and Kerry had offered an ear should one be needed again. But Jacobine had the feeling that Kerry provided support to a lot of people, and might be overextended. Unlike Fran, Kerry didn't have a spouse, adult children, siblings, or in-laws to sustain her in her support of friends. Kerry shouldered a significant load herself, and indeed, was still in the process of wrapping up her cousin's estate.

24

Jacobine's neighborhood held a celebration of Greg Stevenson's life during the monthly meeting, a gathering which more typically featured brief reports from the police about minor thefts, accountings of plans for socials and alley clean-ups, and discussions of sidewalk repairs, street repaving, and "sunshine" cards sent to residents known to have married, produced young, lost relatives, or broken bones in the course of a major remodel. Jacobine had not received cards when anyone in her family had died, since she was the only member of her family who had ever lived in the state and so her relatives were not mentioned in the local paper.

Greg's wife Laurie was not at the meeting; it was understood that the viewing and funeral were the only public events she felt able to appear for. Like her husband, she was well-liked in the community, but from this point forward she would rarely be seen. In her absence, neighbors offered recollections of a man much appreciated, a victim of heredity or of the pleasures of the table.

Later that week, Jacobine and her neighbors went down to the nearby funeral parlor for the viewing; hundreds of people had gathered to pay their respects to Greg's wife and siblings, and so a long line formed that wound around the various public front rooms, where photographs of Greg were displayed and tissues and bowls of mints sat at the ready. Jacobine had never attended such a large funerary gathering; she was impressed that Greg, a seemingly ordinary man of no fame, who had only come to this place as an adult, would prompt so many friends, neighbors, and colleagues to stop by, the day before the funeral itself, to bid farewell. She had liked Greg very much, but their acquaintance had been purely a matter of chatting at neighborhood meetings and socials; she couldn't say she had known him well, or he her, and so she felt it appropriate to attend only the viewing and not the funeral. Not that she had any clear sense of funerary etiquette; she had attended only some family funerals and memorials and a small number of memorials for deceased friends. As her friends lived in many different places and did not necessarily know one another, it was not unusual for months or years to go by before she learned that someone in her life had departed. But this, it seemed, was changing.

25

It was proving a rainy as well as a weepy spring. The nearest location for the national Climate March had been postponed at the last minute due to weather, although a fair number of people, including Jacobine, had turned up and stood around for a while holding their signs and chatting. On May Day, Jacobine drove to the state capital again for a rally in support of immigrants, but in this case it wasn't clear whether the initial event scheduled for nine o'clock had taken place or been canceled, nor did she come across anything at the statehouse later in the morning. Finding no information on the scheduled events or their possible cancellation, she went home feeling somewhat disgruntled. If you were going to announce rallies, you ought either to hold them as planned or let the world know that they were not happening.

Later, she wondered whether the announcement had been a fake planted by the Russians to sow confusion; if you went to an imaginary rally where there were no organizers with signs and megaphones, you might not encounter others who had also come, and later you might choose not to go to a genuine rally.

• • •

Also that May, Trump met with the Russians in the Oval Office and revealed highly classified intelligence to the

Russian Foreign Minister and the Russian Ambassador. This intelligence, concerning ISIS in Syria, had been provided by Israel, and concerned a spy Israel had managed to place deep within ISIS. It was information so sensitive that the US hadn't shared it even with many key allies. Yet Trump, in his usual loose-lipped fashion, had blabbed to the Russians. And then he claimed to have "the absolute right" to give top secret information to adversaries like his Russian pals.

26

Yet another day arrived in which Jacobine felt laden with emotion and needed to give time and attention to that. It wasn't precisely sad or happy emotion, although it was closer to sad than happy; it was more like an emotional equivalent to feeling achy from unaccustomed exercise; a kind of full, sensitive, achiness. She might also be reacting a little to having had a tooth fixed that morning, although that had been quickly over, with little pain. But this ache felt deeply seated in her emotions, and she didn't feel up for doing much, so she finally wrote a long and reflective card to Fran's family.

Afterwards, Jacobine lay down and rested half the afternoon pondering emotion and life in general.

27

In mid-May, Cinda and Jacobine met up for a bike ride; Jacobine thought this seemed a better plan than letting Cinda talk endlessly on the phone as Cinda was often wont to do, and she felt relieved to have gained agreement to bike before the call had gone into its second hour. While Cinda had a great deal to say during brunch and when they stopped for beer before going home, she was quieter than usual while they were actually biking.

Listening to Cinda, it was often hard to put a finger on much that in itself would qualify as irritating. Other than babble about doggies, Cinda generally talked about things a person might find interesting or at least tolerable in normal conversation. But it seemed that almost everything Jacobine said was merely a cue for Cinda to chatter further about whatever interested *her*. This meant that Jacobine could participate to some extent in Cinda's ongoing ruminations about whether to buy a trailer, because anything Jacobine had to say about trailers was automatically of some interest to Cinda. On the other hand, when Jacobine mentioned that one of Kerry's colleagues had encouraged her to exhibit her photographs at a small local gallery, the most this elicited was Cinda's comment that she too ought to learn more about using Photoshop because although she had bought the program, she wasn't sure whether she had installed it. Cinda did not ask what Jacobine was photographing or how she approached the medium. Perhaps, of course, this simply meant that Cinda regarded Jacobine as a rank amateur, but if that was the case then she had no excuse for talking about her own equally amateur efforts to design stained glass.

When Jacobine mentioned that she had been asked to contribute a book chapter to an anthology, Cinda did squeal excitedly and say they should celebrate, but then said nothing to elicit any further details about the chapter, the book, the deadline, or any other aspect of the undertaking, and instead almost immediately introduced a completely unrelated topic. She then veered into speculations as to whether Kerry might lose her faculty development money by not spending it soon enough. Since this money was contractually guaranteed to faculty members, Jacobine was pretty sure Cinda had this story seriously confused. If faculty had to spend their money by Friday, then why didn't Jacobine know this, as she still had some remnants left of her own money? She had never previously been required to spend all of the year's money in the same academic year, although as she normally spent it on going to a conference, it was typically soon gone.

"Will you be around this summer or traveling?" Cinda then wanted to know.

"Some of both," said Jacobine. "I'll be going to California for my friend Fran's memorial pretty soon, so I'll be gone awhile seeing friends."

"The reason I ask," said Cinda, "is that your neighborhood has that phenomenal annual garage sale and I'd like to use your house to stage a sale of some of my excess stuff since the pedestrian traffic is so high. I really need to do some downsizing, especially if I'm going to move west when I retire."

"The neighborhood sale will be during the time I'll be in California," said Jacobine.

"Well, do you think you could arrange to leave me the key or something?" said Cinda. "I really want to take advantage of all that great foot traffic your neighborhood gets."

"I don't want people wandering into my garage while I'm away, but I don't mind if you set up a table on the front sidewalk," said Jacobine.

"It would be more than just one table," said Cinda. "I have a *lot* of stuff to sell. I wish I'd been able to sell more of it before my last move."

"Well, there's space in front of the house for more than one table," said Jacobine. "My next-door neighbor says he's going to set up a couple of tables in front of his house, so I'd imagine the two of you could join forces."

"I would need access to your house, though," said Cinda. "My bladder isn't going to hold out all day."

"My neighbor does have a bathroom," observed Jacobine.

"It's not just the bathroom access," said Cinda. "I would need to bring everything to your house the night before and store it inside until the sale. And your living room would be the perfect staging area."

"I don't see why you have to store anything at my house the night before. What on earth are you hoping to unload at this sale? Why can't you just load your car the night before and show up to set up in the morning? I don't think the sale starts until nine o'clock."

"Well, there is furniture I'd like to get rid of as well as books and clothes and miscellaneous stuff, so I'd probably need to make two trips, maybe even three. There's a couch I'd really like to sell and I'd need to drive that all by itself with the back of the car strapped open and a little red flag on the tailgate."

"Cinda, I don't think this is going to work. You're welcome to put up a table or two in front of my house, but you live forty-five minutes away and even if you only lived ten minutes away, I don't think it would be practical for you to cart all kinds of furniture over to my house in the hopes of selling it from my sidewalk."

"The easiest thing would be to display the furniture in your living room," persisted Cinda. "I'd move your couch and coffee table into the dining room and then there'd be *beaucoup* space to show people everything."

"Um, no. Not happening. It's the sidewalk or nothing. Sell the furniture on Craigslist."

"I've already tried selling it on Craigslist."

"If it didn't sell on Craigslist, then I doubt it'll sell in one day on my sidewalk."

"But you have all that foot traffic."

"Look, for all we know it'll pour rain that day. You can use the sidewalk but leave the big stuff at home. Sheesh."

Cinda changed the subject to a mishap that had occurred while her dogs had been at their doggie daycare, and then began to reminisce about a high alcohol content microbrew she had particularly enjoyed once in Wyoming.

28

Jacobine most often saw her neighbor Nathan over the fence when they were both gardening in their back yards, a thing Nathan was more diligent about than Jacobine, as he was only employed part-time. She now made a point of being outdoors in order to have a chance to ask him whether he still planned to set up a table during the neighborhood sale, and if Cinda could join him.

"Yeah, I'll do a table again," he said. "When my mom died, she left a lot of stuff upstairs that I have no use for at all. I wouldn't call her a hoarder, but she liked to collect things and her tastes and interests weren't even remotely like mine." Nathan's mother had lived in the house for many years—it was where Nathan had grown up—and upon her death two years before, he had inherited it and moved in.

Jacobine asked how he was doing, and before long they had launched into a discussion of the various medications Nathan was prescribed for his diabetes and other medical problems. While he was younger than Jacobine and looked superficially healthy enough, he suffered a considerable amount from diabetic neuropathy, probably because it was likely that he had been diabetic for a significant period before being diagnosed. Prior to diagnosis, Nathan had not been much inclined to go to the doctor, but the pain caused by his neuropathy had sent him in search of relief.

"The pain can be severe, but it varies a lot," he said. "It's not just numbness and tingling. Sometimes my feet feel like they're being immersed in boiling water, or being jabbed with pins. Sometimes it feels like my shoes are too tight or are filled with water."

"That sounds horrible," said Jacobine.

"It is. And I can't tell whether physical sensations below my knees are actually hot or cold. I wouldn't know if someone was burning me or rubbing me with ice cubes."

"That sounds dangerous as well as puzzling. What can you do for this?"

"Well, at the moment my doctor has me on a combination of Gabapentin, which is an anti-convulsant but also helps with nerve pain, and Tramadol, which is an opioid. I looked this up and the National Institutes of Health website says these are pretty standard choices."

"What about acupuncture?" asked Jacobine.

"The NIH website also mentioned that as a possibility, as well as laser therapy, which is less studied, but I don't think either of those are covered expenses for me."

"You might keep checking about acupuncture," said Jacobine. "I've heard the military is using it a lot now."

"Yeah, that's a thought."

"Are you on insulin?"

"Not yet," said Nathan. "When I was first diagnosed, my doctor prescribed Metformin to control my blood sugar, but that gave me such a severe case of fecal incontinence that I couldn't go to work."

"Ugh!" said Jacobine. "That's vile!"

"Yeah, it was basically intolerable, I couldn't live like that, so I persuaded my doctor to try other options. We'll see. I had a checkup the other day, and it was generally positive—my blood sugar is going in the right direction since the last checkup. Also, we're going to start a medication that helps the nerves heal, so maybe gradually I'll be able to take fewer meds."

"Do you like your doctor?" inquired Jacobine. "I mean, would you recommend your doctor?"

"Yeah, I think so. I don't see why not."

"I ask because I'm not happy with the one I've been going to. I haven't been happy with either of the GPs I've seen since I moved here. I liked the first one personally, but after a while I concluded she wasn't a very good doctor. The one I have now is a better doctor, but not only does she have a really irritating manner—she keeps calling me Sunshine and telling me to smile—"

"It's offensive to be told to smile," said Nathan.

"Yes, especially when I'm at the doctor's office and am unlikely to be feeling particularly perky. But not only that, over time I've found that she's incredibly forgetful, which affects her ability to treat me. She's always telling me that before I leave, the nurse will give me some shot or other—for example my tetanus booster—and then she forgets to send in the nurse and I forget to ask on the way out. And then every bloody time I go in, she tells me I should have a colonoscopy. Well, I had one right on schedule after I turned fifty and it was normal, but for some reason she has never managed to get this entered into my record, so she is constantly telling me to get one and I'm constantly reminding her that I won't need another until after I'm sixty."

"My doctor hasn't shown any sign of being unusually forgetful," said Nathan. "Which is good, because I'm somewhat absentminded myself."

"As am I. It's a normal human trait, but not one I want in my doctor."

"Well, I can ask him if he's taking on new patients," said Nathan.

"If you feel he's a good doctor, I'd definitely appreciate that," said Jacobine.

29

School had been over awhile by the time Jacobine got in the car and headed west to attend Fran's memorial and see other friends. As she pulled into her first motel along the way, in a small town beside I-70, the radio brought news that a bomb had gone off in England just as concert-goers were leaving the Manchester Arena after a big concert, resulting in widespread panic and multiple injuries and fatalities.

On that first night on the road, she had no sooner taken her bag into the motel room than she could hear the manager and another man shouting at each other in the parking lot just outside her door. She couldn't make out just what it was about—was the manager simply trying to deal with a belligerent drunk who had annoyed other guests? Or did it relate to the fact that the manager, like so many motel staff of late, was of Indian or Pakistani origin and therefore a possible target of racist abuse? She considered calling the police, but didn't see a number listed by the phone, and the altercation didn't sound like a 911 emergency.

Checking her email instead, she discovered that Nora McCann, who had been in the same graduate program, had died that morning after attempting suicide earlier in the month. It was distressing news indeed. Jacobine had always recognized that there was a lot wrong there, without knowing any of the details; it was just something

Nora exuded. Jacobine had come to like her, but Nora had always struck her as a profoundly sad, angry, and bitter person, although it had appeared that she was doing better recently than in the past. Claudette, another grad school contact, indicated there was a lot of anger about the suicide among Nora's friends. Jacobine was angry too, but not to the degree Nora's closer friends would be.

A few days later, a white supremacist on a Portland MAX train ranted hate speech at a teenager in a hijab and her African American friend; when three other riders confronted him and formed a barrier between him and the girls, he stabbed two to death and slashed the third.

It was a strange time to be on a road trip contemplating life and death.

30

Jacobine and her friend Penny went together to the memorial for Fran, which was held at the Berkeley Rose Garden and was rightly described as a celebration of Fran's life. Few of their mutual friends were able to attend, and Penny hadn't known Fran very well, but still there were various familiar faces in the crowd; Tamsin attended, whereas Marina and Lili Ann could not. And after all, Fran had known so very many people from so many different areas of life, for instance becoming close to many of her children's friends. One of these served as the master of ceremonies, leading the group in various blessings and reminiscences.

Afterwards, Fran's family members thanked Jacobine for her sympathy card—she had put a lot of thought into it and was glad they'd found it helpful.

"Losing Fran," she told them, "has made me keenly aware of all the ways in which she nourished not just me but countless other friends, in so many, many ways."

On the way back to Penny's apartment, Penny and Jacobine began to think over ways in which they might become more like Fran. Jacobine didn't exactly feel she needed to make a list. She could count things she was already aware of doing and simply try to do them more, like being a wise and compassionate mentor to her students and the museum interns. It wasn't important whether an action was easy or hard for her; the important thing was whether it was beneficial. But she felt she needed to make a better effort.

Meanwhile, Jacobine's neighbor Nathan emailed some photos of the neighborhood sale, noting that Cinda had told him she'd arrive at six in the morning but didn't get there until seven. Jacobine replied that that was typical of Cinda.

• • •

With the memorial attended, there were other friends to consider. There were several whom Jacobine always saw when visiting California; others whom she saw on perhaps every second or third visit; and still others whom she saw rarely if at all, keeping in contact primarily by Christmas card or Facebook. This time around, Jacobine emailed several she did not normally see on her California visits. One, Marcus, was a former co-worker she had been out of touch with for more than thirty years, but with whom she had recently been back in touch and whom she thought it might be good to see again. She had been meaning to try to see him for several years now, but always forgot when actually making travel plans, because they were not in regular contact of any kind. During most of their friendship, things had been good between them, but Marcus had a tendency to be moody, and one day long ago he'd been so pissy to her that Jacobine had stopped seeing him at all and for many years had thought of him as one of her few ex-friends. But it had probably been one of those moody times and would have blown over in a day or two if they'd seen each other again promptly. So, as they were back in touch, she wanted to see what he was like now and talk over their past. However, Marcus replied that while he wanted to see her, he was going to be out of town during her visit.

Jacobine was sorry about not seeing Marcus—she was feeling their old connection strongly just now, missed the energy they had once had of being young and ambitious twenty-somethings in San Francisco. She was not having much luck making plans with some of her other friends, either, but for some reason Marcus was the one whose absence caused her the most regret this time around.

• •

Among those she always saw at least once, however, were Nola and Ramon, who worked at the San Francisco Public Library. So one evening she went over to their flat to sit, as the three had so often done over the years, at the kitchen table and talk. Library problems took up the first hour or so of the conversation, as Nola's branch had had to call the cops that day on a patron who was spitting, throwing things, shouting, and generally terrorizing the staff and patrons.

"It was not his first time doing this, either," added Nola.

"That's awful," said Jacobine.

"At the Bernal Heights branch, we get something like this about once a week," said Nola. "It's really exhausting."

"Do you get much of this too?" Jacobine asked Ramon, who was currently deployed at the Main Library.

"Oh, Main has that kind of thing every day, except that since Main is so much bigger, it's not quite as noticeable to everyone. There are a lot of people who are psychotic, of course—the library is a relatively safe place for them to spend the day—and then there are an increasing number of people who are on totally bizarre new drugs that make them much more aggressive than the addicts we used to see in past years. Heroin addicts don't tend to be all that aggressive, whereas these people will yell and throw things and threaten the staff and other patrons."

"Our main library has trouble with heroin and opioid addicts OD'ing in the bathrooms—even parents who OD in the children's room bathrooms—" said Jacobine, "but I haven't heard that it has a major problem with aggressive patrons. There's a lot of security in our main library now, though. Every time I go, I see security guards hanging out watching for signs of trouble."

"We've definitely got ongoing aggression at both Main and the branch libraries. It simply reflects what's going on in the streets these days," said Ramon. "And it's not just the addicts. For instance, San Francisco has a big trans population, and the trans people who get into trouble at the library for whatever reason get really angry when staff address them with the wrong pronoun."

"I suppose that's not too surprising," said Jacobine. "It can be tricky. I've noticed that these days it's becoming more and more common in academe to sign off emails with your preferred pronouns, and to put them on name tags and so on."

"Yes, and we try to be sensitive, but it doesn't work very well when you've got somebody who looks like a Hell's Angel but goes by Ruby, or whatever—in the library you can't go around asking people for their preferred pronouns, because so many patrons are tough ex-cons who're just out of prison and just looking for an excuse to vent their anger at the world."

"This does make our library's problems with adults OD'ing in the children's section bathrooms seem like mild stuff," agreed Jacobine.

"Well, heroin is a problem across socio-economic classes," said Ramon. "Back when I was at NYU I had students who were on heroin; both Columbia and NYU had a serious undergraduate heroin problem, never mind that most of the students came from wealthy families. But now there's Fentanyl and who knows what else out there."

They moved on to discussing whether full employment was desirable. Ramon argued yes, whereas Nola and Jacobine argued no on the grounds that it hadn't worked under Communism and there would always be some people who would simply refuse to work.

• • •

For reasons partly professional and partly personal, Jacobine also drove over to San Francisco's Golden Gate Park to see a huge exhibition at the de Young commemorating the Summer of Love. She enjoyed the exhibition and its displays of posters, photographs, and costuming—she took note of ways in which some of these were displayed, especially the use of lighting and darkness and color to accent some of the displays—but at the same time found it disconcerting to see so many elderly people in bourgeois attire examining these relics of their youth and either trying to recognize Jerry Garcia in photos or talking about what they did or didn't listen to back then. Naturally, many people who'd been young in 1967 were going to look old fifty years later in 2017, but Jacobine would have liked to see more people who were still visibly counterculture. To be sure, many of the older attendees might still be politically active, might be working for peace and to save the environment, without feeling a need to dress differently from the general population. You just couldn't tell by looking at them, or even by listening to most of them.

31

On Jacobine's way back from California, she made a point of staying with friends and relatives who lived along the way, which was always a pleasure on these road trips. But in the Rockies, staying with her cousin Lee, the cold air in the makeshift guest bedroom, which prevented the air mattress beneath her from warming at all during the night, ultimately fully woke her and prompted her to pull on pants and sweater. At the same time, she began to have a strange sensation—not, unfortunately, new for her—in which she felt like she'd swallowed a stone.

Jacobine had not had one of these attacks in several years—what a shock to be afflicted with this again! Usually the sensation had been localized in the center of her chest; this time it began lower on the right and then began pulsing downward from her breastbone to her navel. As she waited for it to subside, she reminded herself that when she saw Nathan's doctor she must ask about this, as it didn't sound like anything she had read about heartburn or gallbladder attacks. When she had tried to ask her last doctor, the result had been less than useless—Dr. Fell had claimed that Jacobine needed to describe the sensation better. Apparently it wasn't good enough to say it felt like she'd swallowed a stone, because Dr. Fell had then brushed off the problem with the assertion that she couldn't diagnose anything that vague, just as she'd always ignored Jacobine's queries about sometimes waking up nauseated, claiming that everyone sometimes eats things that disagree with them. Well, but why was Jacobine waking up nauseated so much more frequently now than she had during the rest of her life?

And so she lay fully dressed on her cousin's chilly air mattress, covered in blankets and a down comforter, with the air in the room feeling about fifty degrees, while her digestive tract suffered one of these painful episodes and she wouldn't be able to warm up in the shower until Lee and Jordan vacated their bedroom, because the house had only one shower. But gradually the pain subsided, and she felt normal enough by the time Lee and Jordan woke up.

• • •

Further along her way, Jacobine arrived at an attractive coffee purveyor just in time for the fire department to arrive to assist an elderly customer. The patient seemed calm enough, but they'd brought in a stretcher, and five paramedics began to interview him while the rest of the customers kept an eye on the situation.

The paramedics then began to give an IV drip, and got the patient hooked up to an array of lines. The patient checked his phone for something or other, stood, and the paramedics helped him get comfortably situated on the stretcher.

Jacobine thought the man looked at least ninety, but in command of himself. He waved to his friends as he was wheeled out the door, and she thought, *This looks like it could have a happy ending.*

32

Back at home for the Fourth of July, Jacobine went to Cinda's for a cookout, taking along her neighbor Nathan since he had no other plans. Initially, Cinda's main topic was her garden, and the garden looked lovely indeed, with its mix of flowers, shrubs, and mature trees, but while at first Jacobine enjoyed being led around the yard and shown Cinda's latest horticultural acquisitions, she soon concluded that she did not require an exhaustive account of each plant and where in the yard it had been transplanted from or how it had most recently been pruned or fertilized or, indeed, what had infested it of late.

Meanwhile, Cinda said almost nothing to draw Nathan into the conversation beyond occasionally commenting that the dogs liked him. When he did begin to say something, she cut him off with some new ramble of her own. Jacobine found this annoying and tiring and had the feeling that Nathan did too although his manners were impeccable.

"There's a very attractive house on your block that I saw during the neighborhood sale," commented Cinda as they finished their meal. "One of your neighbors is fixing it up to sell, so he showed me around."

"Huh, I wonder which house?" said Jacobine. Nathan's attention was on the dog he was petting; having inherited his own house, he did not take great interest in which houses were under renovation.

Cinda said, "It's unusual for your neighborhood in that it has a long double lot that would be ideal for the dogs. Most of the yards in your neighborhood just don't have enough space for dogs."

"Quite a few of the neighbors do have dogs, though," remarked Jacobine. Both dogs and cats were common in her neighborhood, although many of the cats were feral and subject to repeated efforts to trap and spay or neuter them.

"Those are mostly smaller dogs," said Cinda.

"I wouldn't say that," said Jacobine. "There's not a shortage of huskies or pit bulls. I see them around quite regularly."

"But you've got that neighbor who does corgi rescue, and there's also the neighbor with the two dachshunds," asserted Cinda.

"There are dogs of almost all sizes, short of St. Bernards, in my neighborhood," said Jacobine.

"The house I was looking at, which is really lovely and which your neighbor is almost done renovating, actually has a yard big enough for my dogs, which makes me really feel tempted to put in an offer on it," said Cinda.

"I thought you wanted to live closer to work," said Jacobine. "Otherwise you wouldn't have sold your other house."

"Oh, I couldn't take that commute anymore!" exclaimed Cinda. "But even with the amount of work I've done on the house and yard here, this place is just never going to be as nice. It's not nearly as good a neighborhood, either. My other neighborhood was conservative, but this one is full of Trump supporters."

"That's uncomfortable," agreed Jacobine. Nathan, who had nothing to contribute to this conversation because he had never seen Cinda's former house and was not keeping track of the dog population in his and Jacobine's own neighborhood, gazed at the yard and sipped his beer.

"I'd really like to move back out west when I retire, but I'm not having much luck landing a job at any of the places I'm applying to. So maybe I should just buy that lovely place in your neighborhood and go back to doing the longer commute for a little while before I retire."

"You hated that commute," said Jacobine.

"I could do it again for a little while," said Cinda. "I'm really fed up with having Kyle for a boss, and the sooner I can retire, the better."

They continued to sit in the garden drinking beer for a while after eating, but eventually Jacobine suggested that she and Nathan ought to head home, and Cinda did not press them too strongly to stay.

Back in Nathan and Jacobine's neighborhood, it was possible to see the city firework display rather nicely from certain choice locations; each year Larry Muller and Mardon Smith hosted a viewing party on their extensive lawn, providing root beer and diet cola while attendees brought lawn chairs, blankets, and cans of beer. Nathan liked the idea of seeing the fireworks from a different location than from directly beneath them at the city park, especially as he didn't care for all the patriotic music played at the park, so when it got dark, he and Jacobine got their folding chairs and drinks and walked over together. They said hi to several neighbors, including of course Larry and Mardon, settled their chairs in an advantageous spot, opened their drinks, and sat back to enjoy the evening.

33

Soon after that, Jacobine drove to Chicago for Nora McCann's memorial. She was surprised to find that the memorial was being held at a church, and at first assumed that that was Nora's parents' idea, but the pastor spoke about what an asset Nora had been to the congregation and how Nora had described herself as "religious but not spiritual." Jacobine, like the pastor, had heard many people describe themselves in the opposite manner; in fact Jacobine occasionally said it of herself. However, she had not expected Nora to call herself either religious or spiritual. Nora was a person who had always struck Jacobine as entirely secular, an intellectual, analytical person who was probably an atheist. Well, or an agnostic; Nora tormented herself about various things and so it was likely she had been a tormented agnostic who couldn't decide whether any gods existed. Perhaps Nora had found a degree of comfort in routine religious observances, in the manner that people suffering from obsessive-compulsive disorder find or at least seek comfort in specific actions such as rechecking the stove or performing a personal ritual to ward off disaster. It was even possible that Nora herself had suffered from OCD, but if she had, it hadn't been to a degree noticeable to her acquaintances.

Nora's religion was not the only surprise. Nora's mother was also somewhat unexpected, although in terms of personality she seemed quite normal and unremarkable, as was perhaps appropriate for the occasion. But Nora hadn't looked exactly white, and Jacobine recalled that Nora had hated it when people asked if she was Chinese. Nora had at some point in the past posted a Christmas-time photo of her father on Facebook, and he had looked like a freckly redhead, so Jacobine had supposed that Nora's straight black hair and slightly Asian skin tone were maternal contributions, possibly Native American. But Nora's mother arrived at the church with pale European skin and wavy light-brown hair, so for the first part of the memorial Jacobine found herself wondering if Nora had been adopted. However, Nora's mother then began to speak about how Nora's birth had been so difficult that Nora had had to be resuscitated, and how having had whole decades of Nora to treasure was cause for gratitude and rejoicing. Jacobine's ruminations now veered away from wondering whether Nora had been adopted to contemplating the fact that people whose births had been difficult often struggled later with depression and related problems. Still, she didn't like to attribute Nora's suicide to Nora's almost not having survived her birth, since many other things could ultimately have been more significant.

In the course of the memorial, Jacobine also learned other mildly surprising facts about Nora; not that it was unexpected to learn about new aspects of a person one hadn't been especially close to. All the same, she hadn't expected to learn that Nora had been an accomplished clarinetist. And then it was also somehow odd to hear testimony from Nora's sobbing recent friends that she had turned their lives around. From *what*, they did not say.

As Jacobine sat in the pew with her graduate school cohort, she mused that although she had never claimed to know Nora very well, it wasn't as if they'd barely known each other either. She had known a bright, articulate, tightly wound person who drank a lot, swore constantly, and seemed troubled by much of what life throws at a person. Nora had been most comfortable with the intellect, but unsatisfied by it. She had seemed both steely and brittle. However, in recent years Jacobine hadn't seen much of Nora as Jacobine's job had taken her away from Chicago, while Nora had remained.

Jacobine was pleased to see several of their old professors in attendance. Her former advisor spoke about the quality of Nora's scholarship, which prompted the question of what Susan might say were she to speak at a memorial for Jacobine. Nora's own advisor was not in attendance; indeed, Jacobine noted that none of the male faculty seemed to have come. But many of their graduate cohort were there, although none of them spoke up during the program, only more privately during the reception that followed.

As the reception wound down, people began to talk about going for drinks and began saying it was nice to see Jacobine, in a firmly go-away-now sort of way. The younger members of their graduate cohort had known Nora much better and knew each other much better than they knew Jacobine, so she decided not to call any other local friends, and drove home in a ruminative mood.

34

Jacobine had now arranged to have her first appointment with Nathan's doctor, which she was almost looking forward to; but it turned out that there were numerous things to be done before she actually went, so she and Nathan sat discussing the sheaf of forms that Jacobine had been sent to fill out before her initial visit. They both found it somewhat strange that the clinic requested patients reveal a great deal of data about gender and sexual identity and practice.

Nathan said that he had asked whether this information went on his public record, as in the current political climate, with some doctors trying to refuse to treat gay patients, he didn't want that in his paperwork.

"I can see where it's medically useful to know this sort of thing, but I don't like to have it in my paperwork either," said Jacobine. "And all the questions doctors ask—at least it's usually in the office rather than on forms—that are less straightforward than they initially appear. Like 'are you sexually active' and 'how many partners have you had,' which are just not simple to answer unless you've had a pretty limited sex life."

Were Nathan and Jacobine sexually active people? They both felt that "not right now" was the most correct answer. Besides, how active was "active"? It seemed neither had had sex in at least a couple of years, which seemed disappointingly inactive.

"That's not exactly how we want to see ourselves, is it—" said Jacobine—"as people who go that long without sex? Without sex with a partner, anyway." Jacobine didn't find solo sex very interesting, nor did she think it probably counted as sexual activity for the purpose of the medical questionnaire.

• • •

At the clinic the next day, hoping that Nathan's doctor would prove suitable for her as well, Jacobine could hardly say she enjoyed listening to the soap operas and ads for diarrhea medications that blasted forth from the waiting room TV; this was even worse than the medically focused television that had played in her previous doctor's waiting room, which was at least somewhat educational. Anyhow, it was just not possible to read with all that noise. Why couldn't there be a normal traditional rack of magazines to occupy patients who hadn't brought anything of their own?

And it was hard to believe that she was getting closer and closer to sixty, which had once been what seemed like old age and an age at which people routinely died. At least nowadays death at sixty was not really the norm in the industrialized world. Death at sixty was a bit on the early side now. On the other hand, Jacobine's neighbor Verna had told her that very morning that her disabled daughter had finally died at the age of forty-five. Verna said her daughter hadn't been expected to live beyond forty.

But once out of the waiting room and meeting the doctor, Jacobine was reassured. Dr. Ng was pleasant, asked sensible questions, and arranged for the phlebotomist to do appropriate blood tests for a person of

Jacobine's age and medical history. Thyroid, cholesterol, diabetes, Vitamin D, those sort of checks.

"I think I'm generally very healthy," said Jacobine, "but I do get various mysterious random things, like the morning when I woke up dizzy and so unbalanced that I had to crawl downstairs and have a neighbor drive me to the doctor. Luckily that only lasted a day. More often I've had strange episodes where I feel like I've swallowed a stone. I haven't had one just lately, but it's definitely something that recurs from time to time. The most recent episode was a few weeks ago."

"We can see if we can figure out what that is," said the doctor. "It might be acid reflux, depending on where you feel it."

"Well, it can be at various locations. Sometimes I have it about here—" she gestured at her chest—"and sometimes it's further down, on the left or right. The same sensation, though. And sometimes I wake up in the middle of the night feeling nauseated, but I don't throw up."

"We can start with a medicine for acid reflux and see if that does the trick. If it doesn't, we'll see what else might be helpful."

35

The FBI conducted a predawn raid at the home of former Trump campaign chairman Manafort, seizing tax and banking documents and other materials related to the special counsel investigation of Russian meddling in the 2016 election. Senator Blumenthal of Connecticut, a member of the Judiciary Committee, called the search "a significant and even stunning development," saying that such raids were usually characteristic of "the most serious criminal investigations dealing with uncooperative or untrusted potential targets." He elaborated that "a federal judge signing this warrant would demand persuasive evidence of probable cause that a serious crime has been committed and that less intrusive and dramatic investigative means would be ineffective."

Trump continued to make wild statements about a wide range of topics. He threatened to rain "fire and fury" on North Korea, comments which were cheered on by an evangelical preacher who claimed that "God has given Trump authority to take out Kim Jong Un." In contrast, Jeffrey Lewis, a nuclear nonproliferation expert, said, "The question is: What did Trump think he was saying? My guess is he didn't think about it at all. That's the problem."

Threats of a different sort came a few days later when hundreds of MAGA-hat-wearing white supremacists carrying torches and Confederate flags descended upon the city of Charlottesville. They aimed to stage a giant rally to "take America back" and protest the planned removal of a statue of Robert E. Lee, but were met by counterprotesters chanting "No Trump! No KKK! No fascist USA!" In the afternoon, a young racist from northwest Ohio drove his vehicle directly at the counterprotesters, then reversed at high speed, killing one and injuring many others.

The governor of Virginia declared a state of emergency and told "all the white supremacists and the Nazis who came into Charlottesville today: Go home. You are not wanted in this great commonwealth." Trump, whose presidential campaign had emboldened America's racists, avoided condemning the white supremacists.

Jacobine signed petitions denouncing white supremacists and their hate and violence, and RSVP'd to attend one of the hundreds of candlelight vigils being organized to commemorate the victims.

•   •   •

And so, the day after the attack in Charlottesville, Jacobine and Nathan walked downtown to their vigil.

"That's where I used to go for HIV testing," remarked Nathan, pointing toward a large building across the street.

"It's been a long time now since I was last tested," commented Jacobine.

"I haven't been there in a long time now," said Nathan.

"A minor advantage in our lives of miserable celibacy, I suppose. No need for HIV testing."

"I've gone in for self-love," declared Nathan sarcastically.

"That's all very well, but personally I prefer to have a second person involved." Sex, thought Jacobine, was one of the only areas of life where she found her own company boring or limited. But these days thoughts of sex were few compared with feelings of outrage.

They were pleased to find the local vigil to be well attended; several hundred people raised their candles aloft in the square. After the speeches, the group was directed to do a march through the streets, during which Nathan and Jacobine ran across one of Jacobine's colleagues, Elise, and her husband. Nathan and Elise's husband proved to know each other slightly and had friends in common, so they had a long conversation as the group paraded through the downtown with their mostly expired candles.

"The events in Washington these days are just too numerous, too crazy, too unbelievable," lamented Elise. "How can Trump pretend that there are 'very fine people' in the KKK?"

"I know," said Jacobine. "He's such an obvious racist. Not to mention that we could be launched into a nuclear war with North Korea at any time."

"Everything is absolutely insane," said Elise. "It's exhausting."

"I sign petitions, read some of the news, and hope that Trump will be removed on account of his obvious mental instability and incompetence. It's distressing to live in a country that was once internationally admired and is now an object of combined derision and fear. It's horrifying how many people actually support Trump and his attitudes."

"Yes," said Elise. "I never expected Nazi Germany to rise anew in the US."

By now, this kind of conversation was typical across the United States.

36

Toward the end of the summer, Cinda called—late in the day—to suggest meeting to bike before dark. Jacobine was hesitant—it would take her at least an hour to drive to the bike trail proposed by Cinda—but she assented and, as Cinda arrived, unusually, in a relatively timely manner, they managed to do about an hour and a half of biking plus supper.

"I'm feeling really broke again after having to fix my car in order to drive to Idaho for my vacation," said Cinda, "and then Marlow had his accident and I've had to spend thousands of dollars on his vet bills and then what happens but I find out that the car needs all kinds of additional expensive work—new struts and I don't know what all else."

"That's really unfortunate," said Jacobine.

"Of course, my salary at the museum is diddly-squat, like most museum salaries, and furthermore Kyle expects me to come in on all sorts of nights and weekends because I'm on salary instead of hourly, but you know my salary isn't enough to compensate for all that extra time; obviously if I were hourly they'd have to pay me overtime."

"Yes, obviously," said Jacobine. "It's normal to come in for the occasional special event or whatnot, but hardly to come in for huge amounts of extra time."

"It's not like Kyle is coming in for all this other stuff himself, all this docent-related stuff outside normal working hours, or giving gallery talks seven days a week."

"Tell him you can't do all of it, that it's exploitive."

"I wish I'd hear back about that job I interviewed for in Eugene. That would be such a cool place to work! What a perfect job, just like it was precisely tailored to fit my skills and expertise."

"You still haven't heard anything?"

"Not a peep! And it's been quite a while since I interviewed."

"That's not sounding promising," said Jacobine, who concluded that the museum in Eugene had surely hired someone else by now.

Cinda then began a long and rambling anecdote about running across her realtor at a wine tasting and hearing all about the realtor's friend's attraction to a man who had had a messy divorce that wasn't quite final.

"For whatever reason, the guy's ex-wife really wanted to screw him over, so the judge made him sell everything he owned at auction and give half to the ex."

"As if that's usually a reasonable way of extracting cash from someone," commented Jacobine. She generally took a dim view of punitive divorce settlements, although of course there were times when such measures might be warranted.

"Well, I don't know the details, but it made the guy tell my realtor's friend that he couldn't imagine ever being in a serious relationship again," said Cinda. "But she was still hoping he might change his mind, even though things weren't looking that promising."

"Yep," said Jacobine. "Not an unusual story, I'm afraid."

"So next," said Cinda, "in the meantime she ran across a note that this boy she had known in junior high had given her when she went off to boarding school, about how he wished he could kiss her."

"Boarding school!" exclaimed Jacobine, who was a product of public education, as were most people she knew. "Your realtor's friend went to *boarding school?*"

"Apparently," said Cinda. "Anyway, while she hadn't been in touch with him since then, she somehow happened to know how to contact him, so she did and he told her he still wanted to kiss her."

"O-o-o-kay."

"It turned out that he was actually quite wealthy— owned several houses, etc."

Jacobine's expression was not one of approval.

"He invited her to travel with him," continued Cinda, "but she said no. He invited her to visit him in the Caribbean, but she said no. Then he invited her to visit him in Maine, and she agreed."

"Right," said Jacobine, for lack of any more intelligent comment to offer on this development.

"She packed light, but she included a slinky dress that all her friends just raved about, because he'd asked her to bring along something nice to wear in case they went out to dinner."

"Slinky dress, check."

"So she got there and everything seemed promising, but he needed to meet with some bigwigs, so she was going to need to dress up for this."

Jacobine supposed, at this juncture, that Cinda's story was leading toward the couple meeting the Obamas or somebody exciting like that, but Cinda proved not to know who these bigwigs were, or indeed anything whatsoever about them. They were just generic bigwigs.

"She was supposed to dress up for this," said Cinda, "dress up, to the hilt, so she put on this dress that all her friends thought she looked so stunning in. And then—can you imagine—"

"No, I can't," said Jacobine.

"Her host told her she had terrible taste in clothes!"

This was not an outcome Jacobine had foreseen. "What did she do?"

"She said 'Says you!'"

Jacobine laughed. "What did she do then?"

"I don't know what she did apart from saying that. During the rest of the visit, her host made clear that he was hoping to sleep with her even though he'd told her she had bad taste in clothes. But meanwhile, she was thinking about the other guy again and how maybe he was warming up again."

"Was he?" inquired Jacobine, although this was of no great interest to her.

"I don't know," said Cinda.

"Did she sleep with her host?"

"Oh no, it sounded like she was pretty turned off after he insulted her dress."

"Hmm." Jacobine never quite gathered the point of the anecdote; perhaps Cinda never quite finished it. Jacobine did like that the woman had said "Says you," but apart from that, she felt that this story lacked much point and that the woman was probably far too eager to find a man with money. She wondered what exactly had prompted Cinda to recount this tale.

37

A few days later, Jacobine was twiddling her thumbs waiting for Cinda to arrive at the bike trail. They had considered biking on a trail closer to Jacobine's house for a change, as after Cinda had moved further away, their biking tended to occur nearer to her house than to Jacobine's. But this time Cinda had come up with the notion that they ought to park at opposite ends of a section of trail and do some sort of relay of driving that, according to Cinda, would enable them to bike a longer section of trail than if they started at one end and turned around.

Jacobine could not see how Cinda's proposal would be better than biking one way together and turning back, or how for that matter Cinda's idea would even be feasible—if they parked their cars at opposite ends to unload the bikes, then surely they must bike to the center from those opposite ends, not both bike from one car to the other. Anyway, Jacobine said, it didn't make sense to her.

"People do this all the time to extend the distance biked," asserted Cinda. "They cart the bikes on one car and drive forward to the other."

"But then you're carrying the bikes forward, not riding them. And it still doesn't make any sense to me for *two* bikes and *two* cars," said Jacobine, who could not picture this at all. "Maybe for a multi-bike trip and one person with a truck?"

Cinda said "Well, then how about instead we meet in the middle where we usually do and have brunch first?"

"Fine," said Jacobine, since although this meant she would yet again drive for nearly an hour and a half on country roads to get to their small-town starting point, they had at least found a good place for brunch which was around the corner from a good place for sandwiches and beer.

And so, as was so often the case, Jacobine was here close to on time while Cinda was more than half an hour late—this time, she claimed, because she was delayed by a Labor Day parade. *She is just incapable of arriving anywhere on time*, mused Jacobine as she located a park bench. *I'm often slightly late to meet Cinda since there's no point in being early where she's concerned. Oh well. I have a book and with luck she won't be more than an hour late.* Still, she looked wistfully at the many bicyclists flowing up and down the trail and wished she too were on her bike under the tree canopy rather than sitting out in the open trying to be visible from all of the adjoining parking areas.

"Well, I finally got word that I didn't get that job I interviewed for in Eugene," said Cinda when she arrived. "I probably didn't use enough jargon once I got as far as the onsite interview. You know how some people just spout jargon right and left as if the average person is going to understand it. Personally, I prefer to be understood."

"Overuse of jargon is indeed tiresome," agreed Jacobine. She wondered whether perhaps Cinda had, rather, been late to the interview.

But they pondered jargon for a while, and then Cinda said "I'm still feeling really pinched for funds given all my recent vet bills. Since I'm having such a hard time moving on to a better job, I've decided that the best option for paying off these vet bills is to get a roommate to move into my second bedroom. Do you know of anyone who might want to do that?"

"You really want a roommate?" asked Jacobine, who did not know any such person.

"Well, not particularly, but I have to do something about these bills, and if I got the right roommate, it could be a good thing for both of us. I haven't really had any friends at work since Julie left, and my neighbors are all Trump supporters so I can't talk about much with them. Besides, with the right roommate I wouldn't have to board the dogs when I go out of town for a few days."

"That's true," said Jacobine. "I just wonder how easy it will be to find the right roommate."

"Oh, I don't think it should be all that hard. I'm not planning on charging an arm and a leg, and there are lots of students in town. In fact, I've got an Australian grad student coming by tonight to take a look."

"I hope you told her about the dogs."

"Oh yes, she says she loves dogs."

"Well, then she sounds like she could be suitable," said Jacobine, but she wondered whether loving dogs necessarily translated to wanting to live in a household that revolved around three large rambunctious "doggies" who were prone to barking. And then there were Cinda's three cats as well, but nothing revolved around them.

Not too surprisingly, Jacobine learned the next night that the potential roommate had not expressed great pleasure when all three dogs leaped onto her as she entered the house, especially as she was wearing white pants at the time. Love of dogs only went so far with most people.

38

Somewhat against her better judgment, Jacobine next agreed to go canoeing with Cinda. It wasn't so much that canoeing itself was against her better judgment—she was eager to try it and thought the canoe should contain at least one experienced person. But she had stupidly left her phone at home, so she had no idea how late Cinda would be—because Cinda was always late—and the thought of another afternoon with Cinda monologuing about doggies and everything that was wrong with her job was not easy to look forward to, with the way Cinda generally rattled on with seldom a pause. If Jacobine herself started a topic, it could only develop in a direction that interested Cinda and provided her with an opportunity to hold forth for the next ten to twenty minutes.

So Jacobine stationed herself at a picnic table in view of the canoe rental office and settled down to enjoy being, if not precisely in nature, being in nature's vicinity, under big spreading trees and surrounded by families and church groups of rambunctious children. And before long Cinda was twenty minutes late despite the fact that the canoe rental office was surely closer to her house than to Jacobine's.

"There you are!" exclaimed Cinda at last, stomping up vigorously.

"Yes—did you get lost again? I'm afraid I left my phone at home so I wasn't sure what your situation was."

"I was only lost for about fifteen minutes. That was after I had an escaped doggie to track down, Orson thought he should take advantage of my opening the front door to go romping down the street. He was very naughty. And then I didn't see you when I got here, so I sat down on the other side of the building and read a book for a while before looking around."

Jacobine had investigated the area thoroughly before choosing her picnic table, so she said "Well, I got here an hour ago, so I've been observing the youth of today and tomorrow learning how to put on life jackets."

"There are quite a few of them, aren't there," said Cinda, turning to look.

"There were even more half an hour ago, but I think we can still get a canoe."

Once paid and lifejacketed, they joined about twenty others in a repainted school bus to go upstream to the launching area. Jacobine, who had always been under the impression that canoeing was a tricky skill involving excellent balance, was mildly apprehensive about whether they might capsize their craft getting in, but these plastic rental canoes were broad and sturdy, and one stepped aboard with the aft end resting on the riverbank, so although boarding was a tippy experience, there was little danger of falling in, let alone capsizing. Once both women and their plastic-encased belongings were situated, a canoe employee gave the craft a shove and they were afloat.

"He was rather attractive, wasn't he?" said Cinda.

"The canoe guy?" said Jacobine. "I didn't notice."

"He reminded me of my college boyfriend," said Cinda.

"Ah," said Jacobine.

"Brad and I used to take every chance we could get to get out on the water in a canoe, kayak, or raft," said Cinda.

"Nice," said Jacobine. "I don't think I ever heard any of my college friends doing that. I suppose some did, I just didn't know about it."

"Brad was like a water dog," said Cinda. "He was on his high school water polo team."

"Ah," said Jacobine again. She envisioned a Portuguese Water Dog in a high school swimming pool. Or maybe Brad was a Labrador Retriever, or an Irish Water Spaniel, or a Chesapeake Bay Retriever.

"Brad was also a pretty good hiker. But let's get our paddling underway before we drift too far."

"Yes, you'll need to show me the proper technique," said Jacobine. "I've only paddled on lakes before, in a plastic kayak, not canoed in a river."

"You'll pick it up fast," said Cinda, and she began to demonstrate the basics, which Jacobine did indeed grasp without too much trouble. "We won't need to paddle constantly, since after all we're mostly doing a lazy float downstream. But now and then we'll need to steer to avoid rocks or shallows or those other canoers. Right now, for instance, I'd like to get us a ways away from all those other canoers who got off the bus with us."

"Excellent," said Jacobine. "Full speed ahead. What a gorgeous day!"

"I'm so glad we were able to get this scheduled before the canoe rental places close up for the season," agreed Cinda. "Once school starts, their schedule starts to contract, and of course some weekends it rains, so next thing you know the season is over."

"The weather seems just perfect today." And it was—warm and sunny, but with many shady areas from the trees that lined the river.

From there, conversation was mainly about trees, water, and other boaters, except for when Cinda caught sight of someone's dog, which inevitably redirected her from whatever she had been talking about, midsentence. But altogether, it was a lovely respite from politics, the refugee crisis, and climate change. One could feel as if it were any time in the past two hundred years when adults and children, in families, pairs, and solo, paddled North America's rivers for pleasure on summery afternoons. It was a bit like stepping into a painting by a member of the Hudson River School, or by some other nineteenth-century American painter with a penchant for the scenery east of the Rockies.

Altogether, Jacobine concluded that evening, it had been a lovely weekend—in their own personal bubble, to be sure, given the devastation that hurricanes Harvey and Irma were causing further south, not to mention the numerous other calamities and general bad stuff going on around the world. But at least a few humans had been enjoying a life of general happiness and innocent pleasure all weekend. Jacobine had gone to the farmer's market Saturday, roamed about with her camera, stopped in at Kerry's current exhibition, biked a bit around town on her own, and had now gone canoeing and eaten a nice dinner along the river with Cinda.

39

By some miracle, that year Jacobine entirely missed out on any reminders that it was the anniversary of "9/11." What a relief it was not to have to listen to grave comments about this horrible yet over-fixated-on event! Other countries suffered terrible attacks on a regular basis; why did Americans think they were so special? Why was 9/11 seen as unusually tragic? It invariably disgusted Jacobine that the cruel deaths of so many civilians and rescue forces were made an excuse for flag-waving and American alleged exceptionalism.

But in less than a week, Trump dubbed the North Korean dictator "Rocket Man" in a Sunday morning tweet just before he was scheduled to attend the annual UN General Assembly. The North Korean regime had recently done its biggest nuclear test to date, an explosion far larger than the atomic bomb that had devastated Hiroshima in 1945, and while this was by definition worrisome, it had evidently prompted Trump to want to one-up Kim Jong Un. In speaking to the UN, Trump threatened to "totally destroy North Korea" and again called Kim Jong Un "Rocket Man" as he raved about "loser terrorists."

As it happened, the North Korean delegation was seated in the front row, mere feet from the podium.

"The United States has great strength and patience, but if it is forced to defend itself or its allies, we will have no choice but to totally destroy North Korea," said Trump. "Rocket Man is on a suicide mission for himself."

Never mind that people all over the United States now wondered whether Trump would annoy the North Korean dictator into bombing American cities.

40

But one could not think about North Korean missiles all the time, any more than one could countenance thinking about Trump all the time. Delighted with the success of their afternoon in the canoe, Cinda and Jacobine were contemplating getting out on the water again while they still could. But as September progressed, the weekend weather hadn't been ideal for another day of canoeing—although Jacobine thought overcast preferable to hot and sunny—so Cinda came up with the idea of going to the local Renaissance Festival.

"I've concluded that festivals are what Midwesterners do on the weekend," she said. "Think about it—every weekend there's some kind of festival. The German Festival. The Celtic Festival. The Greek Festival. The Hispanic Festival. There are Bluegrass Festivals. Bourbon Festivals. Harvest Festivals. There are Pawpaw, Marigold, and Covered Bridge Festivals, for Pete's sake—how do you have festivals about covered bridges? And then there are Lesbian Festivals and Fish Festivals. I mean, it just does not stop. When do these people have time to mow their lawns?"

"Maybe they don't have lawns."

"This is lawn country," said Cinda. "It's the land of the riding mower."

"True enough," said Jacobine. "I'm sure my neighborhood's turn away from lawns is a minority position for the region, although I've noticed that there's a move toward planting shortgrass prairie areas among some of the cities."

"That's interesting," said Cinda, "I hadn't noticed that. But dogs need lawns so that they don't completely dig up the rest of the yard. It's not so hard keeping the doggies out of my rosebushes, but they get into everything else."

"Kids like lawns, too," said Jacobine. "But in moderation. Kids and dogs like to have stuff to explore besides their lawn space. I loved figuring out little secret shelters in the shrubbery."

"Well, are you up for checking out the Renaissance Festival?"

"Sure. I used to love going to the Renaissance Faire when I lived in California. I'm up for seeing what the 2017 version of the Renaissance Faire might be like."

"I've never been to a Renaissance Festival," said Cinda, "but it seems to be a big annual event around here."

"It is, it's huge, I just haven't gotten around to going."

But there was no getting Cinda in gear to actually *go* to something she had proposed—at half past ten, her status was that of having cleaned house, gone out for a walk, and needing a shower. Meanwhile Jacobine, who had thought they might want to get to the site around ten, had been frittering away her morning in an attempt not to get involved in anything too time-consuming or that required her full attention. So a bit of laundry, a bit of weeding, but mostly just checking the news online between messages. The Sierra Club wanted her to tell her legislators to vote against the coal bailout. The *Washington Post* revealed that Hurricane Irma had devastated one of the U.S. Virgin Islands, with the Coast Guard ferrying "dazed tourists" to cruise ships headed for Miami and San Juan. A mysterious creature washed ashore in Texas during

Hurricane Harvey was tentatively identified as a fangtooth snake-eel. The nuclear test done by North Korea on the third of September had apparently sunk an eighty-five-acre area on the peak of Mount Mantap above the tunnels typically used for North Korea's nuclear tests, indicating that the hydrogen bomb was probably close to 250 kilotons and thus by far the largest yet at the site; North Korea had followed up with a statement that it would use nuclear weapons to "sink" Japan and "reduce the U.S. mainland to ashes and darkness." Two Motel 6 locations in Latino neighborhoods in Phoenix were reported to have been sending data on guests to Immigration and Customs Enforcement at five o'clock each morning, resulting in at least twenty arrests. A high school student near Spokane was killed trying to stop a school shooting. And the vice president had claimed that "President Trump's leadership inspires me every single day."

Soon it was nearly noon, and Jacobine's whole morning had disappeared into the interstices between text message updates. She wished that someone would finally hire Cinda for a job in some other state so that she wouldn't be tempted to make plans to do things that ended up eating her entire day. *The payoff is always less than what I hope in entertainment value and I get so annoyed with her perpetual lateness.*

And so they didn't actually arrive at the festival until two o'clock, when the weather was hotter and there was more threat of rain. Although Jacobine felt angry all the way there, she went into a more neutral mood once she arrived at the dusty impromptu parking area and began to see people streaming toward the entry gates. Cinda was soon visible too.

They bought their tickets and looked around before entering.

"I didn't expect entrance to cost this much!" exclaimed Cinda as she put away her credit card. "Haven't we paid more like five dollars when we've gone to the Bluegrass Festival?"

"It wasn't this expensive, I know that," said Jacobine, "but these Renaissance-themed fairs are a bigger deal. They aren't cheap."

"And look at all the people coming in costume! I certainly didn't expect that," said Cinda, pointing in the direction of a heavily costumed group that included a nearly giant fellow in vaguely medieval-looking armor beside a gaggle of young women in long skirts and tightly cinched bodices.

"Oh, costume is a major part of Renaissance fairs," said Jacobine. "I always used to long to dress in more period-appropriate garb than just the generic long skirt I sewed myself in junior high."

"I'm not seeing anything that looks very authentic to the period," observed Cinda as they proffered their tickets at the entrance and began to take in the scene.

"No, I'd say people aren't too clear on the concept," agreed Jacobine.

"It looks to me as if people don't know the difference between Renaissance and Medieval, or for that matter Renaissance and Middle Earth. Look at all those people wearing elf ears!"

"That's very odd," said Jacobine. "Nobody ever used to wear elf ears to the Renaissance Faire. At least, not that I remember. Medieval stuff, yes—after all, I don't suppose peasant garb changed remarkably between the two periods."

"The elf ears are kind of cute, they're just not from the Renaissance."

"Exactly," said Jacobine. "I'd be up for wearing elf ears for some other kind of event. Halloween, of course, but maybe there are more elf-appropriate holidays than that."

"Well, anything goes at Halloween, and elf ears would certainly be more imaginative than some of what people wear."

As they wandered about, they found the festival to be extremely commercial—mostly booths selling this or that, with not very much to see and hear in the way of performance, although they enjoyed some juggling and hurdy-gurdy. Not that after a while they didn't start to enjoy some of the commerce as well, just that they felt some resentment at having paid over twenty dollars each for the opportunity to shop.

Jacobine recalled that in the early 1970s she had admittedly enjoyed buying hand-made herbal soaps at the Faire, and that twenty or so years later she had bought some jewelry. She merely remembered the Renaissance Faire of old less for its commerce and more for the performances and the majestic procession of a splendidly gowned Queen Elizabeth with her courtiers; in her teens she had been enamored of all things Renaissance and also all things Medieval.

And so this time Jacobine bought a pair of elf ears and a Battenberg lace parasol, as well as getting her hair braided, while Cinda bought a fabric porch swing with a drink holder for her beer—none of which, obviously, exactly suggested the Renaissance. They had gradually moved into a state of suspending disbelief regarding historical accuracy.

The young woman who braided Jacobine's hair, working this particular venue for the first time but a veteran of other Midwestern sites and a proud member of a lengthening line of Ren Faire workers going back to her great-uncle or so, lamented that these days the musicians were all older because her own generation was uninterested in playing early music and folk music. The hurdy-gurdy player, an elderly enough woman taking a break from performing nearby, agreed with her and said younger people today just weren't interested in learning period performance. That fit with Jacobine's own observations, which were that of late people seemed uninterested in learning what was actually known about how early music had been performed, and were focused instead on how to perform it in some catchy new way. And while she wasn't opposed to finding new ways of performing old music, she thought you also needed to know what you were departing from.

So in the end the afternoon was simultaneously mildly pleasant and rather disappointing. After returning home, Jacobine simply reverted to feeling low, and lay down on the rug with her head on her beanbag chair, feeling generally incapable of dealing with life. While it hadn't been a bad day, she wondered if perhaps Cinda battened on her emotional strength. Cinda never seemed perturbed by Jacobine's occasional sharp comments or the way she had almost entirely lost interest in holding up her own end of the conversation.

She could, obviously, stop spending time with Cinda, but they had common interests. She thought, *I know a fair number of people in the area, but hardly any of them are people I actually do anything with—I have dinner with Kerry or Beth once in a while, I see my neighbors at our neighborhood events, I talk with colleagues at union meetings and museum events. That's about all!*

41

On the first of October, a sixty-four-year-old man fired over 1,100 rounds of ammunition from his suite on the thirty-second floor of the Las Vegas Mandalay Bay Hotel onto a crowd of concertgoers at the Route 91 Harvest music festival. He killed 58 and wounded 422, with the ensuing panic bringing the injury total to 851. About an hour later, the shooter was found dead in his room from a self-inflicted gunshot wound. No one ever learned exactly why he had shot so many complete strangers.

That fall Jacobine was taking a digital photography class taught by one of Kerry's colleagues. Josh gave some interesting assignments—Jacobine was enjoying them— and at the moment they were working on one called Evidence, in which they put together a small photographic series documenting evidence of something or other—or in which they created fake evidence to photograph. Either real or faked evidence was entirely acceptable, but a rationale was required for whatever one photographed. As Jacobine had quite a few other things to do that month, inventing a uniquely creative and artistic project was unfortunately not at the top of her to-do list, so she had chosen to photograph cityscapes featuring billboards. Consequently, she was roaming the area near downtown evenings and in the rain in search of options for the five required prints. An electronic billboard half a mile from her house, photographed in a downpour from under her umbrella, provided gleaming signs relating to Suicide Prevention, Foster Parenting, and, finally "Pray for Vegas."

At first Jacobine wondered if this last was a religious effort directed at saving Sin City, but then she remembered the shooting. There were so many mass shootings in the US these days that you could not be expected to keep track, but this was such a huge one... Yet if everyone was supposed to pray for Las Vegas, where were the signs about the storms that had just devastated Puerto Rico? Right after Hurricane Harvey hit Texas and Louisiana, there had been signage offering sympathies about that, so why not after hurricanes Irma and Maria as well? Or was it enough that Trump had tossed packages of paper towels to Puerto Rico's survivors?

On this walk in the rain, she didn't see any of the usual signage about child abuse, addiction, or welcoming immigrants, but then there weren't that many billboards on this particular route—in the past she had seen a plethora on these topics. She wasn't entirely leaving out commercial advertisements from her project—earlier, in dry weather, she'd photographed a restaurant sign, a sign about electricity, and a sign recruiting truck drivers. Signs advertising insurance, personal injury lawyers, and medical plans were also rife near downtown, especially along the railroad tracks. But she'd have to see what worked well as a series.

42

Jacobine and Cinda sometimes attended a Bluegrass Festival in the fall, but this year Cinda hadn't responded to Jacobine's inquiry—perhaps she was working that Saturday, or had a veterinary appointment—so Jacobine ended up going alone. The festival was held in a large rural park full of mature trees—maybe even ancient trees, although that seemed unlikely in this part of the country— with the performers and audience occupying a small grassy clearing with a few picnic tables and outhouses near the parking lot. Jacobine had brought a folding chair in order to have some back support, which she missed when sitting on a blanket as many of the audience did; she set this up near where some other older attendees had put up clumps of folding chairs, so as not to get in the way of anyone's line of sight. And as usual at this festival, she realized she should have brought warmer clothing; the air was just a bit cool and damp, nice weather of the autumnal kind, and the option of more layers would have been pleasant.

As she sat and listened, it occurred to her that it was a mildly curious thing to attend a music festival alone in 2017. Not because it was unusual for her personally—she had always gone to many things alone as well as with friends—but because in this year she was more aware of how much time people (herself included) spent looking at electronic screens of one sort or another. People worried that conversation was becoming less and less common, that children were growing up texting rather than engaging face to face, and indeed companies were already developing robots to be "best friends" for kids and the elderly, a notion which Jacobine found bizarre and troubling. On the one hand, new technologies always caused anxiety—Jacobine knew that people had once expected train travel to cause brain damage. Still, despite her admitted attachment to her laptop, she believed that humans needed to spend more time in nature. Indeed, the main thing she didn't like about her laptop was that she'd never had one with a screen that was very visible outdoors, and therefore all of her computer work was undertaken indoors. Not that the climate in her part of the Midwest encouraged her to be outdoors much anyway, as it was either miserably hot, uncomfortably cold, or insects bit incessantly. And that made her grateful for the cool fall weather at the Bluegrass Festival.

But she was aware of the fact that, although she didn't use her cell phone all that much, she spent much of her time on the laptop—writing, checking email, doing miscellaneous work-related tasks, looking at Facebook, looking things up on Google, doing some genealogy, and watching the English, Irish, Australian, and South African episodes of the television program Who Do You Think You Are. She'd gotten somewhat out of the habit of just hanging out observing her surroundings.

And so she was pleased that while here and there she could see a few people checking their phones, overall the Bluegrass Festival was a low-key, sociable event. Families came, groups of friends stood around talking, people stood or sat on folding chairs or lay on blankets; they roamed about, drank beer, got plates of food. It was a nice little festival on the grass, surrounded by tall trees.

Jacobine thought it would have been neat to have gone to something like this as a child. Her family had done quite a few different things, from museum visiting to traveling across the United States car-camping in the National Parks, but they hadn't gone to any outdoor music festivals. It was enjoyable to watch the kids here, and even the dogs, like the attractive puppy that was vigorously wagging its short tail not far from her.

Once she'd thought all of this, Jacobine nonetheless turned her phone on to check for messages, and almost immediately one from Cinda came through asking if there was food at the festival. Jacobine replied that there was, so Cinda responded that she was just three miles away—although that might merely mean that she wouldn't arrive for another forty-five minutes.

But Cinda arrived pretty quickly, and they enjoyed themselves. Cinda had had a phone interview with another museum, this one in Seattle.

"I'd really like to get this job," she said. "This is a once-in-a-lifetime opportunity and in a part of the country where I'd love to live, even though it's so expensive."

"Well, let's hope for the best, then," said Jacobine.

"One thing worries me a little, though," Cinda continued. "It wasn't clear to me whether they did a phone interview with every top candidate or if it was due to one person being unavailable for the on-site interview."

"Surely they'd do the same type of interview for all candidates," said Jacobine. "That's what we do—you can't do phone with one and in-person with another, it's not fair to see one person's gestures and not the other's. Either you see what everyone looks like or you see what no one looks like."

"Ideally," agreed Cinda. "Not everyone adheres to ideal interview practices."

"Wouldn't it be a red flag about the job if they don't? Do you want to work someplace that can't do something basic like that right?"

"Well, I already work in a place that gets a lot of things wrong. This museum may be doing all their interviews by phone, it just sounded like maybe not. If they offer me the job, I'm taking it. I mean, *Seattle!*"

43

Jacobine was attending a retirement planning seminar at the university. As she'd signed up late, she hadn't received her top choices of sessions, meaning that much of what she heard was proving to be a review of familiar topics, or topics that didn't relate to her situation, or alternately was material that she didn't understand. She then moved on to a session in which she learned first that one could invest tax-deferred money in a 457 account, and then that a 403(b) could be even better because one could put more into it each year and it would not be accessible to creditors. Jacobine mused that whether this distinction mattered for her was a separate question—was she actually making enough to skim off thousands of dollars pre-tax to tuck away into such an account? And was she likely ever to be pursued by creditors?

The speaker began to talk about annuities and how it wasn't smart to put all your eggs into one basket. This made Jacobine hope that he would swiftly move onto something less basic—people were beginning to slip out the back of the room as presumably they, too, already knew that you shouldn't put all your financial eggs in one basket if you could help it. And if you worked for a university, you might not earn all that much, but you probably did earn enough to have more than one basket.

The speaker then brought up what he called the four percent rule. He advised against withdrawing more than four percent of total investment per year during retirement, a piece of advice that sounded vaguely familiar to Jacobine. One should first make withdrawals from taxable accounts, he stated, then from tax-deferred accounts such as traditional IRAs and 403(b)s, and finally from Roth IRAs. But of course there was also the matter that once one reached the age of seventy and a half, the IRS required one to begin making withdrawals from what he termed "qualified" retirement accounts.

By this time, Jacobine was about ready to fall asleep. She knew that it was important to learn how to prepare for retirement, but she found all of this financial advice terribly dull. If you were eligible for full Social Security at sixty-five —and for most of the audience it was surely *after* sixty-five because how many people in the audience were born before 1943? anyone that old was well past sixty-five by now—then you had very few years in which to fuss about the correct order in which to withdraw from your various hypothetical retirement accounts. Basically, you withdrew, from your taxable accounts, four percent of your total invested hoard—for what? three years or so? Then you moved on, taking the required disbursements from your so-called qualified retirement accounts. Jacobine thought she grasped this well enough, but it was quite another question whether she would have saved enough by the time she retired to follow any of these precepts, and furthermore, there was no guarantee that the world's financial markets would not crash in the meantime and destroy whatever she had managed to invest. The market might be rising with wild abandon in this first year of the Trump presidency, but you could not expect that to continue. Even in more normal times, you had to recognize that markets rose and fell in see-saw fashion. What if you were one of those poor suckers who needed the money right when the market was at its lowest? And if you were someone like her, you might be putting in the most money when the market was climbing (since that was when you finally had money available to invest), only then to see everything go poof. Trump might start a nuclear war, or the melting ice caps might inundate New York, or solar storms might fry the world's electrical grid. The dystopian possibilities were endless. It seemed unlikely that she would be able to enjoy a simple retirement in which travel, gardening, hiking and biking, books, and conversation with close friends (all of whom currently lived far away) were the mainstays and in which protests and social activism were a spice rather than practically a main dish.

44

Jacobine lived within walking distance of the local German club, so as it was advertising Oktoberfest, she wandered over for supper. The club didn't serve food on a regular basis, but for certain holidays and festivals its volunteers cooked masses of schnitzels and wursts, which were available along with quantities of sauerkraut, potato salad, and German beers. Like most white Americans, Jacobine had some German ancestry, and as her family was originally from the Midwest, she had grown up eating a certain amount of German fare, although in general she did not think German-American cooking was as good as German cooking in Germany.

When she arrived at the club, she found numerous people dining to the accompaniment of an oompah band, but there was nothing else going on. She got in line and bought a schnitzel plate, but soon discovered that the schnitzel was overcooked and tough. Apparently the American cooks hadn't learned about pounding the meat to tenderize it. Or maybe pork schnitzels would simply never be as good as veal schnitzels. Maybe it was time for her to become a vegetarian, since most of the time she ate like one.

After finishing her meal, Jacobine remained in her seat to finish her beer, but she was suddenly joined by a very soft-spoken man of around her own age, neatly but blandly dressed in chinos and a short-sleeved plaid shirt with windbreaker, whose words were nearly incomprehensible when the band was playing. He didn't have a plate of food, he just came over and said something about how someone over at the food line had told him that she could tell him all about the club and its activities.

"That's strange," said Jacobine. "I'm not a member, so there's only so much I can tell you. But since I live around the corner, I do know a certain amount. They have a chorus and a genealogy group and they have folk dance classes of some kind. They put on a German Festival in the summer and have a Christmas market in December. But that's about all I know."

This didn't seem to satisfy the man; he continued to ask Jacobine about the club, but there was really nothing further she could offer to enlighten him. He was polite and nicely dressed, so she didn't feel alarmed, but she could barely hear him, so it was an effort even to maintain this minimal level of conversation—she kept having to ask him to repeat himself. She supposed he might have been attracted to her and noticed she was alone—he appeared to be a decently healthy specimen, and wasn't wearing any rings. Yet while she hoped eventually to meet someone in the area who was attracted to her, her sole reaction to meeting this person was a desire to end the conversation and go home. She felt, rightly or wrongly, that here was one of those Midwestern whitebread people that one might like well enough as a neighbor but who went to church, was probably a Republican, and showed no sign of having any common interests beyond a yen for German cooking.

45

A few days later, Cinda called, saying she was at the local pub. Since Jacobine hadn't seen her since the Bluegrass Festival, she felt she couldn't decline to meet, which was a good thing, as it turned out Cinda had just had one of the dogs euthanized.

"I'm so sorry!" exclaimed Jacobine. "You loved Marlow so much!"

"He was such a sweetie, such a loverboy," lamented Cinda. "It's so hard to say goodbye, but it was time. He was in too much pain."

"It's hard to make that final decision."

"I'll miss him so much... what a joy he was... I'm having that new IPA. What're you thinking of having?"

"Oh, I suppose I'll have the brown ale."

"I like sitting here at the bar. You get such a good view all around. So often when you sit at the bar in a place, you can only really see the other side of the bar."

"I suppose," said Jacobine, who found cheerful observations about bars to be a peculiar chaser for grief, even if there was little more to say about the hole Marlow might leave in Cinda's life.

"Is that house in your neighborhood still for sale? That one I looked at during the yard sale?"

"Well, I don't know, but I doubt it. Houses in this neighborhood usually sell pretty quickly."

"You should ask your neighbor about it. The one who was working on it. There was still work to be done fixing it up, so maybe he hasn't sold it yet."

"I'm pretty sure it's been sold," said Jacobine. "You looked at it months ago."

"Well, it would be nice if it was available," said Cinda. "I'm so fed up with working under Kyle that sometimes I could just scream. He's so passive, and he's also passive-aggressive. The director isn't any help either. She just goes along with whatever he tells her. I told her when we interviewed him that he wasn't the right person for that job. We had a much better candidate—everyone liked her—but no, we had to hire Kyle instead and now I've been stuck with him for two whole years. At this point he's been there almost as long as I have! And the pay I'm getting is laughable. Museum salaries are just pitiful."

"Mmm," said Jacobine.

"I'd love to get that house in your neighborhood, and it'd probably be somewhere in my price range," said Cinda. "If I could get that house, it'd be so much easier for us to get together for drinks like this! You're the only person I know in this part of the country that I can bike with! Kerry needs to spend so much time in the print studio. But on the other hand, I'm very interested in a job that's come up in Denver. That would be a real coup, very exciting, I'd be helping design exhibitions, which is certainly not something I get to do much of in my current position even though it's something I've done before and am pretty good at if I do say so myself. Plus I'd be within spitting distance of the Rockies!"

"Well, that sounds like it could be your dream job," said Jacobine encouragingly.

"Yes, it really would be. But housing is so expensive in the Denver area! I was looking around online and it's just hideously expensive, plus in many parts of town the commute to work would be miserable. Denver has some really bad traffic."

"True," said Jacobine. "I've driven in some of it and it's no fun."

"Exactly. But still, it would be a fabulous job. And I have the qualifications for it."

"Well, then you should go for it. See if you can get it."

Jacobine was glad she could be there for Cinda, although she felt that Cinda monologued excessively about her job. On the other hand, for once Cinda actually asked about her research and they talked about that for several minutes before Cinda changed the subject back to Kyle and how he spent meetings looking at his cell phone.

•   •   •

Arriving home, Jacobine skimmed her email.

"Big corporations don't need more tax cuts—they need to start paying their fair share."

"A 62-year-old grandma is serving life in prison."

"Did you know that October is lesbian, gay, bisexual, transgender and queer (LGBTQ) history month?"

"Activists Splatter Red Paint on Roosevelt Monument at American Museum of Natural History."

"Who was the most important black labor leader?"

"Latest footage from the Rohingya crisis."

"Declawing cats is brutal and wrong!"

"Curate your space with decorative plates and bowls!"

"The New Yorker reported that Donald Trump made a 'joke' about Mike Pence wanting to 'hang them all' in reference to LGBTQ people."

There was also an odd message from her mother.

> "I am wondering if you have survived the traumas of the past couple of weeks. Please, just a short note to let us know that you are OK. Mom."

Jacobine had no clue what her mother thought was going on—while Jacobine had had a lot of work to do lately, she hadn't suffered any traumas. Yes, she'd complained about this and that, but it was all only normal work stress, not trauma. Uncle George had had a stroke recently, but he was recovering, so she hadn't been traumatized by that. For that matter, even if he died, she wouldn't be traumatized, although she'd certainly be sad. And national events continued to be pretty wild, but might be leading toward the end of Trump's presidency, which would be a huge relief. It was just odd because her mother didn't usually throw around words like "trauma" lightly and she sounded as if she thought Jacobine might be injured or suicidal, which was hardly the case. Being unhappy about the state of the world might be depressing, but not *that* depressing, even if you were also wondering how the rest of your life was going to turn out. It wasn't as if she was a Rohingya refugee corralled in a camp, or a Syrian fleeing across the Mediterranean on an overloaded boat. Life in the United States, for a person with a reasonably secure and even generally rewarding job, was not stressful beyond her capacity, even under Trump.

46

Checking the clock after lying awake for a very long time, Jacobine noted that it was half-past four in the morning. Evidently she should have taken a sleeping pill; there was a gallery meeting to attend in a few hours. But she didn't like to take sleeping pills. She found it offensive that since becoming a professor, she seemed to need them, often, in order to be able to do her job.

It was complicated, this matter of medication. Part of what sometimes kept her from falling asleep was thoughts about her students, most of whom seemed to be either on medication—for anxiety, depression, autism, who knew what else—or in need of it; or they were caring for one or more family members who had cancer or serious psychological problems. She often felt surrounded by people who were suffering in one way or another, not that all of them revealed this.

And while suffering was part of the human condition, it didn't seem like it should be part of the human condition for everyone to be medicated all the time. It was one thing for Nathan to have to take an array of pills to control his diabetes, including sleeping pills, because the pain from his diabetic neuropathy could be severe. There was no doubt about his diagnosis, and in fact he came from a family with many diabetics; his mother had died of diabetic complications.

It was possible that Jacobine's students who were anxious and depressed came from families prone to these feelings. She assumed that some of them did. But it was also much noted in the world at large that American college students now tended to be medicated for anxiety and depression to a degree not seen in past decades. And no one seemed to know quite why—were they under more stress for legitimate reasons, or were more people with these problems able to go to college now than in the past, or were they not eating right or not getting enough exercise, or were they brought up in ways that kept them from learning how to cope? Jacobine had no idea. In her undergraduate days, people had certainly experienced stress, were situationally or even medically depressed, but they were not mostly on meds as far as she knew. They were mostly able to manage, and lived to go on with life after college. Then again, people did tend to use a lot of illicit drugs in those days, and it was common to drink to some extent, so it could be argued that Jacobine and her peers were self-medicating.

And although Jacobine associated her present insomnia largely with teaching and menopause, it was not entirely a product of this period of her life, it was just that in this period of her life she was sometimes unable to sleep at all, which had a serious effect on her job performance. As far back as she could recall, she had always lain down, closed her eyes, and begun thinking about something— preferably something interesting, even exciting. In childhood, it had been thoughts of adventure—of being Heinrich Schliemann or Austen Layard and uncovering lost cities. In adulthood, it had usually been thoughts of sex and ideas for projects. While her mother took the view that it was a problem if one hadn't fallen asleep after twenty minutes in bed, Jacobine could not agree. She had not made a practice of looking at her watch during the night for the majority of her life, but she doubted that she had usually thought about any of these things for less than twenty minutes per night.

However, being tense at night, feeling like she just couldn't get to sleep, or being unable to stop thinking about her students and their problems, was different than enjoying pleasant reveries. She didn't want, for instance, to lie there all night seeing Bay Schmitz sitting in her office wanting to hug her because she was going to give Bay a D instead of an F after Bay missed the exam because she wasn't fully supplied with her meds and her boss upset her, causing her to forget she had an exam. Nor did Jacobine want to lie there all night hearing Mirnetta Josten worry that she was failing because she didn't know how to get what she knew onto paper, and thinking that in any case Mirnetta clearly suffered from a disability of some kind, possibly autism.

Of late there had been numerous memes circulating on Facebook about "empaths," which various people of Jacobine's acquaintance claimed to be—rather like how everyone these days imagined themselves to be introverts, including Jacobine's hyper-extroverted intern Annamaria Longo. Both introversion and being hyper-empathetic were paraded as cause for simultaneous lamentation and pride. So for instance Jacobine had seen a fairly dismally drawn cartoon of a figure going about its day absorbing more and more darkness from every person encountered (apparently curing *them*), then finally going home and being greeted by the dog, who dispelled all the day's accumulated darkness. Jacobine supposed that there were indeed times when she picked up people's emotions in that manner, but she was relieved not to feel that this was how she experienced daily life. She believed there to be a qualitative difference between *thinking*, even if rather uncontrollably, about the people around her, and actually absorbing people's misery and *feeling* it like one's own.

•   •   •

Not that anyone in the national government appeared to be either an introvert or an empath, which was perhaps why these labels were so popular among Jacobine's Facebook friends. On the first of December, the dismissed national security adviser Michael Flynn appeared in federal court formalizing a deal with Special Counsel Mueller to plead guilty to a felony count of "willfully and knowingly" making "false, fictitious and fraudulent statements" to the FBI. James Comey, the former FBI chief, alleged that Trump told him to be easy on Flynn, and produced notes quoting Trump as saying "I hope you can let this go." Predictably, Trump soon began to tweet, claiming he had never asked Comey to halt an investigation into Flynn's conduct. "I never asked Comey to stop investigating Flynn. Just more Fake News covering another Comey lie!" he raved before dawn on the third.

"Are you ADMITTING you knew Flynn had lied to the FBI when you asked Comey to back off Flynn?" tweeted Walter Shaub, the former head of the U.S. Office of Government Ethics, in response. With matters under investigation expanding beyond collusion with Russia to include obstruction of justice and financial crimes, many observers saw Flynn's cooperation with the Mueller investigation as a sign that other White House aides, and potentially Trump himself, could be in legal trouble next.

47

Faculty at Jacobine's university attended graduation ceremonies in rotation, so that about every two years she was one of the people representing her department. This time it was her turn to attend Winter graduation, which was a smaller event than Spring graduation, and was the most pleasant time to don her heavy gown and slightly slippery cap. It was also Kerry's turn to attend, so the two carpooled to the university stadium for the pre-graduation faculty breakfast. This was a chance to have some scrambled eggs and bacon and bagels with people one might know from other departments, so they sat with an acquaintance from Sociology and one from Communication, and then were joined by Barry Niven, an Anthropology professor whose course Jacobine had sat in on the year before. She hadn't seen him since the start of the school year and she felt slightly guilty that she hadn't yet congratulated him on a teaching award he had received. She'd also meant to email him to say that she had used some of his pedagogical tips.

Barry seemed in a good mood, so Jacobine asked about his teaching and he spoke about experiments in teaching his largest class in a newly designed classroom that seated everyone in small groups.

"I think it was reasonably successful," said Barry. "I lost no more students than usual, and it made it easier for the weak students to engage."

At that point the announcement came that it was time to don their gowns, so while Kerry had not spoken much with Barry, she helped him figure out how to do his PhD hood—hood design from different universities varied, and hardly anyone wore their regalia more than once a year, so although Kerry, as an artist with an MFA, had no hood of her own, she became the hood arranger and arbiter for the entire table's worth of PhDs.

Jacobine did not particularly enjoy her university's large graduations, although she felt the ceremony was an important one for faculty to attend, a good ritual with splendid costuming. This time around, she felt the event was more appealing than usual. There was no invited commencement speaker (these could be rather iffy, although usually they were alums who had made good rather than famous people who might nonetheless be poor speakers); this time the university president gave the ceremonial address and focused on how the graduates would need to solve major world problems that his own Boomer generation had not followed through to completion.

Jacobine usually found President Schuler's speeches too hearty, too full of folksy Midwesternism, but she approved his emphasis on peace and ecology, and was pleasantly surprised when one of the choral numbers proved to be the spiritual "Down by the Riverside, I won't study war no more." While she supposed it might not appeal greatly to the ROTC contingent, it seemed an excellent choice to her and to Kerry.

●　　　●　　　●

A few days later, Jacobine stopped in at the German club to shop at its Christmas market and have a German supper. The market was busy, filled with tables loaded with German and other goods, some sold by local church groups and others by professional vendors. She looked over the Baltic amber display, but refrained from buying any, as her mother already owned an amber necklace and didn't wear it; she examined the small wooden figures of lively children, gnomes, and animals, which had become so much more expensive than they had been in her youth; she fingered the quilted placemats and wall hangings; looked with interest but no thought of purchase at the beer steins; and finally bought two Christmas ornaments. With that, she joined the supper line.

"I see that they're selling 'Tracht' downstairs," said a woman ahead of her, a person around her own age. "I wonder what that is?"

"Tracht?" echoed the man beside her. "Where does it say that?"

The woman pointed to a sign, and the man said "Tracht... well, it probably refers to tracts of some kind."

"Tracts?" said the woman. "What are those?"

Jacobine intervened here, unable to tolerate further linguistic confusion. "Tracht refers to traditional German clothing. Dirndls and Lederhosen are Tracht."

"Oh!" said the woman. "How interesting!"

This led to further conversation among the three, so Jacobine agreed to join them at a table, as she would have to share a table in any case.

"This is so interesting," said the woman as they sat down. "I haven't really eaten German food before, even though my family is mostly German. And look at this cabbage!" she said, pointing to a small mound of red cabbage on her plate. "I wonder how they get it to be this color? Do you think they use a dye?"

Both Jacobine and their male companion looked at her in some surprise.

"That's red cabbage," said the man.

"It grows that way," said Jacobine. "Haven't you seen it in the grocery store before?"

"I've never seen anything like it!" exclaimed the woman. "It's really pretty."

"Well, you can buy some at just about any grocery store, at any time of year," said Jacobine. "Surely you must have seen it before in restaurant salads..."

"I can't wait to see what it tastes like!" said the woman with great excitement.

Meanwhile, they were joined by another man, likewise of approximately Jacobine's age. She supposed that people of this age—near retirement and somewhat post-retirement—were an important population for the German club's Christmas market, being likelier to have some money and free time, as well as perhaps having more people to shop for than did younger people.

The new man at the table promptly began to talk about his Norwegian sweater. It was a handsome heavy pullover in two colors of natural wool plus a subdued blue that was perhaps from a natural dye source, and everyone duly admired it.

"It was expensive, but a very worthwhile purchase," he said. "It's also very easy to care for. The important thing with this kind of sweater is, you mustn't dry-clean it."

"Really?" said the woman who was unfamiliar with red cabbage. "I thought wool had to be dry-cleaned."

"Not natural wool like this," said the man.

"Most wool is best off washed by hand," said Jacobine.

"Dry-cleaning strips away the natural oils," said the man with the sweater. "It's very harsh and ultimately damages the fibers."

"Dry-cleaning also makes wool much itchier," said Jacobine.

"I never knew that!" said the red-cabbage woman. "I've always dry-cleaned wool."

"I do dry-clean my wool coats and suits," said Jacobine, "but I hand-wash the rest of my wool. In cold water, of course."

The man with the sweater now focused his attention on Jacobine and began to tell her in detail exactly how he washed the sweater; he used a special soap, and never Woolite, but if necessary he could use shampoo, provided it was the right shampoo, one without unnecessary chemicals and perfumes. He provided an astonishing amount of detail about exactly how he washed this sweater, causing Jacobine to wonder how quickly she could make her escape from these people, who while friendly enough were beginning to make her feel bombarded. Was there something about her that invited this sort of conversation? You might have this sort of discussion about how to wash wool with a vendor selling wool sweaters, or with your friends or relatives with whom you also discussed many other things, but why would you fix on such a topic to discuss with strangers met by chance? Did it seem like a good substitute for discussing climate change or literature? She didn't mind a little bit of information about the sweater and its care, but this was far, far, too much.

48

As 2018 dawned, Jacobine pondered the discrepancy between her own generally acceptable life and the situation in the world at large. In her own life, she could be grateful to have a mostly agreeable job where, in exchange for doing useful educational work in the classroom and the museum, she was guaranteed enough money to eat and lead, for better or worse, a middle-class existence. In the world at large, on the other hand, crazy stuff was happening right and left and governments were becoming increasingly fascistic and generally dangerous to all life on earth. According to the *Washington Post*, for instance, in just one thirty-minute interview, President Trump had made at least twenty-four false or misleading claims. How could anyone so lazy, ignorant, and corrupt lead the country? She just had to hope that Trump and his crew would soon be removed from office so that things wouldn't continue to go to hell in a handbasket—or more likely a plummeting jet. Trump, in fact, was madly tweeting "North Korean Leader Kim Jong Un just stated that the 'Nuclear Button is on his desk at all times.' Will someone from his depleted and food starved regime please inform him that I too have a Nuclear Button, but it is a much bigger & more powerful one than his, and my Button works!" Fortunately, neither dictator pressed his button...

On the personal side, Jacobine admitted that she wouldn't mind finding a paramour—someone intelligent and kind who was also a lot of fun. She was tired of celibacy, tired of not having a partner with whom to share decisions, experiences, and (for that matter) house cleaning and maintenance. It wasn't out of the question to meet someone suitable at her age—she had some good examples from among her old friends. If her friend Dave could find his wife Hope after years of certainty that he'd end up alone and impoverished in a residence hotel, and if for that matter her acquaintance the seemingly unlovable Dorsey could finally find his soul mate, there was no reason to assume she herself must be celibate or nearly so for the rest of her life. At the German club, it was true, she'd recently met men who might possibly have been interested in her, but she could not see herself becoming interested in *them*. She'd mentioned this to Nathan, but he had had no definite assessment to offer on men who came and monologued at her; he thought it likely that Midwestern men were awkward about approaching people they were attracted to, as he himself was.

"I think it's a regional characteristic," he said, emphasizing that it was not purely his own nervousness as a gay man approaching men who might turn out not to be gay even if he met them in a gay bar.

But if it was regional, then why did Midwesterners all seem to get married? And those who didn't *stay* married got married repeatedly. She knew that from her cousins.

•   •   •

Distracting herself from such thoughts, Jacobine looked out the window. The view was gorgeous—blue skies above, several inches of snow on the ground. Unfortunately, though, temperatures were so frigid that although

Jacobine wanted to go for a walk, the likelihood of frostbite deterred her—the forecast had suggested that frostbite could occur within ten minutes. Certainly her poorly insulated laundry room was arctic enough! She did plan to attend the neighborhood meeting that evening—assuming she didn't forget, which she often did—so she'd experience the weather then. It was a shorter walk to the meeting than to anyplace else she might want to visit.

In the meantime, she settled down to examine her retirement accounts, which included, along with traditional and Roth IRAs, a brand-new 403(b) created after her day at the retirement seminar, and also an investment account that did not fall under any of the governmentally defined retirement categories, but was simply a good place to hold retirement money in a fairly liquid manner. Jacobine didn't consider herself particularly financially adept, but she didn't regard herself as inept, either. For most of her working life, she hadn't taken jobs that paid much, so she hadn't gathered much of a nest egg, but after returning to school and then getting the combined teaching and museum position, she had tried to make a point of socking away as much money as she could. Although she'd probably inherit something when her mother was gone, it was hardly wise to assume anything about that. Her mother was frugal and had every intention of leaving a useful inheritance, but Jacobine didn't like to ask too much about the specifics—she felt her mother ought to live a comfortable life during the years that remained, not stint herself to provide for Jacobine's own comfortable retirement.

Since Jacobine had only recently learned that as a university employee she could open a 403(b), the equivalent of the corporate world's 401(k), and put a portion of her salary into it pre-tax, it was rather new to her and she wasn't all that clear on the details. She hadn't been sure whether she could only add a $6000 catch-up contribution once, but investigation of the IRS website now indicated that after you reached age fifty, this was an every-year option. Feeling a bit rueful, she now set her monthly contribution to $2000, which was an absolutely enormous chunk of her income. Would she be able to live on what was left? Well, she'd see. Any additional money needed for living expenses would have to come out of her savings.

Jacobine wasn't *eager* to take money out of her main liquid account, as in 2017 the stock market had gone wild and provided a huge return on investment, but maybe she could leave that alone for a few months and let it keep racing upwards—assuming, of course, that the market didn't crash, which sooner or later it would. For the moment, the business world seemed to figure that Trump was just great—and it was true that he'd just given corporations a huge tax break while fiddling with the average citizen's taxes in less promising ways—but she didn't think most of Trump's policies were actually all that business-friendly. Hardly anyone wanted to return to burning massive amounts of coal, and car manufacturers weren't too excited about the prospect of being allowed to return to building vehicles that polluted more than those they were currently making. Likewise, energy companies might not be very environmentally conscious, but their executives weren't all idiots, either, and could see that wind, solar, and geothermal were booming and could be a wise investment. Scotland, she knew, was on target to be fossil-fuel free by 2030 and planned for all of its electricity consumption to be generated through renewables by 2020. In Germany, meanwhile, renewable sources already accounted for thirty-eight percent of the net electricity production. Even in the US, wind and solar were gaining considerable ground and providing new jobs; even in oil-rich Texas, wind and solar were popular. By 2015, Georgetown, Texas, had in fact become one of the first American cities to be considered 100 percent renewable, as it produced more renewable energy than its customers consumed; the city government cited financial stability as the impetus for a focus on renewables.

As she continued to examine the IRS website, Jacobine now wondered whether she had better also open a 457(b). Her permissible IRA contribution was $6500, and with $24,500 allowed for the 403(b), that would come to $31,000—close to half her annual salary! The contribution limit for a 457(b) was apparently separate from the 403(b) limit and in theory she could put $18,500 in a 457(b) in one year. Well, she certainly did not earn enough to do that! First she'd better see if she could handle a full contribution to the 403(b), which seemed unlikely enough.

But provided Trump didn't destroy the US economy and/or the earth, Jacobine estimated that between her investments (late though they were) and inheritance, she should have retirement income.

●　　●　　●

In her calculations about the future, Jacobine also reckoned that it might be a good idea to go to the university's annual Promotion & Tenure workshop. She had been an associate professor for several years, and while it wasn't unusual for people to retire as associate professors, full professors made significantly more money. Therefore, for retirement purposes she really ought to go up for full professor as soon as possible. And as her pension would be based on an average of her last five years' salary, clearly she needed at least five years of full-professor salary to maximize the pension. If she started the process now, it would take the entire next academic year to go up the chain of committee approvals, meaning that if the promotion was granted, she'd be full professor starting in a year and a half. She had the required publications, so it was a question of how her teaching and service were seen.

But then, when she went to the workshop, she learned that because she hadn't told her department chair by the first of the year that she wanted to go up for promotion, she was pretty much out of luck for now. Jacobine was not sure why this requirement wasn't mentioned in the published list of deadlines. She gathered that this particular deadline was not hard and fast; it was up to the chair whether to agree to be told after January first. But while she got along well enough with her chair, she knew that Mark was very conservative in his thinking about when people should go up for promotion. He was always inclined to counsel assistant professors not to attempt to apply for tenure early, and to say that associate professors ought to build an ironclad case for promotion so that those reviewing the file would have no possible excuse for knocking holes in it.

While this was not precisely a wrong-headed approach, Jacobine felt it resulted in qualified faculty waiting needlessly long to apply. After all, once you had prepared your promotion dossier, failure the first time around did not mean that you had to come up with a new dossier from scratch for the next attempt. You just had to take what you'd already prepared and update and improve it, which was not that big of a deal if you were, in fact, genuinely promotable. So it was very annoying that she hadn't known she had to notify Mark by January first, because she knew he would tell her to wait another year.

49

Jacobine was annoyed again. It was apparently time to play another round of "how late will Cinda be?" Beth had mentioned that there was an exhibition of Dürer prints about to close in Cincinnati, so Jacobine had texted her, Kerry, and Cinda about possibly going during the weekend. Cinda had been the only one to respond, and had proposed meeting at the museum around two o'clock. Now, at twenty after, Cinda was only just responding to a "where are you" message, claiming she was having "a driveway moment," whatever that meant. Jacobine hoped Cinda meant she was looking for parking and not that she hadn't left home yet.

And eventually Cinda sailed into the museum lobby, filled with good cheer.

"I love your new glasses!" she exclaimed. "They're so colorful! The shape suits your face well, too."

"Thanks," said Jacobine. "So what was this driveway problem you were having? Were you having car trouble?"

"I was having a driveway moment," said Cinda. "There was this absolutely fascinating program on NPR when I got here, and I just couldn't bring myself to turn off the radio until it was over!"

"Oh," said Jacobine dryly. In her view, the fact that one might often sit listening to the car radio in one's own driveway or garage or in the grocery store parking lot did not make this appropriate behavior to engage in when one had suggested meeting someone at two and the other person then had to text you twenty minutes later to find out what had become of you. Cinda could at least have been the first to text. This did not put Jacobine in a good mood, no matter how enthusiastically Cinda might compliment her on her glasses. Cinda could meet her on time and forgo the compliments.

"Lately I've been having a really hard time getting hold of Kerry by phone," commented Cinda. "Have you had any luck reaching her?"

"I don't know, I don't usually contact Kerry by phone," said Jacobine. "Why not email her? You know Kerry believes in answering email."

"Oh, I can't do that, because I'd never notice if she answered."

"Well, then I don't know what to suggest."

The Dürer show was excellent and they enjoyed talking about some of the prints. So that was satisfactory enough. But nearly the entire remainder of the conversation consisted of Cinda talking about her job, her health problems, where she might move when she retired, and trips she wanted to take. All of which would be perfectly normal and potentially interesting topics if it weren't for that nearly all of it was material Jacobine had heard before and that her main function was to periodically say "uh huh" and "that's unfortunate" and similar brief comments. She was feeling that everything was ultimately all about Cinda, which meant that Jacobine then lost interest in saying much about her own pursuits because so little of anything she might have to say would ever have an opening to emerge.

"Are you doing much photography?" asked Cinda, noticing that Jacobine had brought her camera.

"Yes, for the past year I've been quite involved in it. In fact, I had some pieces in a show recently at the Dunton Street Gallery." True, this was in her neighborhood's annual art show, but since Jacobine planned to submit work to juried shows too, she wasn't going to downplay having exhibited.

"We need to start planning our England trip," said Cinda. "I'm really looking forward to our hiking coast to coast together! I've been putting together more information about routes and how we can have our baggage transported."

"I'm sure it would be a neat thing to do, but I'm afraid you'll have to find someone else to go along on this."

"Oh, but you'd be the perfect hiking partner," said Cinda. "We'd have so much fun!"

"I enjoy hiking, but I really don't see how I can do this with you."

"It wouldn't be difficult hiking. And England is so gorgeous! Think of all the quaint little villages with their country churches!"

"It's not the difficulty of the hiking, although I'm not exactly in shape for weeks of it—"

"And you could see those relatives of yours in Scotland!"

"They are in Glasgow, way north of where you want to hike."

"You could still go up and see them. You've got to do this, it will be just wonderful. Just think, entire days of walking the English countryside!"

The idea of being trapped in Cinda's company for several weeks was becoming increasingly alarming despite their friendship, so Jacobine said, "I don't see how I could possibly fit in such a trip in the next several years given how many other places I need to be for one reason or another. I do need to do archival research in several countries, after all."

"Now, another trip I've been thinking about is Japan. It's been much too long since I've been to Japan! You and Kerry should come to Japan with me, because I could show you around and we could climb Mount Fuji and it would be so much fun."

"I'm not really—"

"Kerry has expressed some interest in going to Japan," said Cinda, "and we could stay in hostels to save money."

"I've sworn off staying in hostels," said Jacobine. "I may not be old yet, but I'm too old to stay in hostels anymore."

"Oh, we wouldn't stay in hostels with all those teenagers sleeping forty to a room. There are hostels with individual rooms, there are elder-hostels. I'm dying to show you both the Japanese temples! And the food—so much of Japanese cuisine never makes its way to America."

"I'm not ruling it out, but Japan isn't top on my list of places to visit, wonderful though it is." Jacobine was afraid she could not summon up any desire in herself to have Cinda show her Japan, especially staying in hostels, which would probably mean having to pack her own towels and possibly even her own bedding. Yes, there were things she'd love to see and do if she ever went, but so many things about Japanese culture rubbed her the wrong way. Hello Kitty and the Japanese obsession with cuteness simply repelled her.

"I'm also becoming very interested in Central Europe," announced Cinda. "I'd really like to go to Prague or Budapest with you sometime."

Jacobine thought *OH FUCK, the last thing I need is Cinda following me around when I'm on a research trip looking at Austro-Hungarian emigration data. If she wants* to spend a couple of days in Prague or Budapest while I'm there, I could take her a few places, but I just do not want to spend more than a few hours at a time with her, it is just too exhausting. She remained silent as she attempted to think what to say.

"I was wondering," said Cinda next, "whether Czech women have unusually large busts."

"What?" said Jacobine in astonishment.

"Large busts. I ask because an old spy novel I've been reading keeps referring to large-bosomed Czech women."

Jacobine asserted, firmly, that Czech women's busts were like any other European women's busts.

Yes, Cinda and Jacobine had enough in common that Jacobine could understand why Cinda had this notion that they ought to travel together, but she was beginning to feel that Cinda was going mad. And, if it weren't that Donald Trump had just about poisoned the word, she'd have said it was sad.

50

That Valentine's Day, a nineteen-year-old gunman with a semi-automatic rifle killed seventeen and injured seventeen more at Marjory Stoneman Douglas High School in Parkland, Florida, perpetrating the deadliest high school shooting in US history. The shooter, an expelled student, fled the scene on foot but was arrested without incident about an hour later and confessed.

Survivors of the shooting were soon among the country's most visible activists on behalf of gun control, but the most prominent of them, particularly Emma Gonzalez and David Hogg, were quickly vilified by gun enthusiasts, while right-wing conspiracy fanatics even called them "crisis actors" and sent them death threats; not long after the first anniversary of the shooting, two of the survivors would commit suicide. The shooter himself, who had previously been diagnosed with several mental health conditions, was well known for expressing racist, homophobic, antisemitic, and xenophobic attitudes; he had said he wanted to kill gay people and Mexicans, and that he hated black people "simply because they were black," and hated Jewish people because supposedly "they wanted to destroy the world." Despite the fact that he had frequently been reported to the police as a potential threat and "school shooter in the making," he had bought his weapons legally.

On February 22nd, President Trump suggested arming teachers to stop "maniacs" from attacking students, and on the following day tweeted, "Highly trained, gun adept, teachers/coaches would solve the problem instantly, before police arrive." Student survivors, not surprisingly, criticized such responses and told politicians to enact stricter gun control rather than perpetually offering mere thoughts and prayers.

51

Jacobine was back in California for a conference, which happened to be conveniently timed to coincide with her spring break, allowing at least a little time to meet up with friends.

In San Diego, she spent one evening with very old friends, which she enjoyed very much. Robin and Jacobine caught up to some extent while chopping vegetables together in the kitchen of Robin and Jon's sixty-year-old ranch-style house, with its original Formica counters and much-painted cupboards; while perhaps Robin would have liked a remodeled kitchen, Jacobine appreciated the fact that Robin and her family were more interested in nutrition and how food tasted than in whether their kitchen had fancy granite countertops, an island, a double sink, and all the latest appliances. Their money went towards books, music, and theater tickets, not renovations.

At supper, they were joined by Rebecca, a mutual friend whose children had grown up with Robin and Jon's three daughters, and conversation grew lively. Robin and Jon's youngest daughter Talia was nearing the end of high school and was full of excitement about plays, dances, political protests, and college applications, an excitement that Robin, Jon, and Rebecca shared, knowing all of the activities and apparently all of Talia's teachers and friends too. Jacobine listened with pleasure to so much happy discussion, occasionally making a comment or asking a question. Had she herself married and borne children, she would have wanted to have just this kind of daughter, this kind of neighbor, this kind of family dinner. Not, of course, that every meal in Robin and Jon's household was so enjoyable or that Talia and her sisters had never been whiny or bratty, but Jacobine knew that her friends had succeeded in building a happy family, and that so had Rebecca and her husband.

Jacobine thus ruminated, as the conversation went on, about how very much at home she felt with them all, how she had for fifty years now enjoyed friendship with Robin and Rebecca and for thirty years Jon too; yet she was simultaneously very aware what a different, even alien, world they inhabited. They all knew the various high school teachers at Talia's school, the current and former students there; they shared a thick web of community and shared a richly enjoyed past, and even, as upper-middle-class intellectual families living for decades in a neighborhood now too pricy to join, they shared privilege of a kind. So although Rebecca was over for dinner because Jacobine was in town, the conversation still revolved around the two families' shared lives, touching only tangentially on Jacobine's life or even on the lives of other mutual friends known to her. This did not happen in a manner that made her feel left out—she was part of the conversation—but still it was all about Talia's school pursuits, the community choir, and college applications.

At the same time, Jacobine noted the curious fact that Robin, Rebecca, and Jon, all looking fit and healthy, nonetheless looked older than she did. Was it because they were parents? Surely not. Their children were all bright and successful, all about as happy as anyone's children could be expected to be. Was it that Jacobine looked abnormally young? But her skin was aging too, just not quite as fast as theirs. She felt melancholy at noticing these small signs of healthy people aging, and sad that she wasn't able to spend more time with her friends. She had cradled Talia's older sisters in her arms, but now they were far away in college. She didn't know Talia's teachers and friends, had never seen her or her sisters or Rebecca's kids onstage in their school plays and concerts.

Jacobine next headed for San Francisco. The notion of getting up at seven to leave by half-past in order to have appropriate time to get to an 11:15 flight—well, that was just disgusting. And back when Jacobine had lived in California, it normally took an hour to fly between southern and northern California, but now the flight time was closer to an hour and a half. Life was regrettably full of minor things that just got worse rather than better over time.

For her first night in the Bay Area, Jacobine was supposed to go to stay with her friend Julia in Berkeley, but Julia, who lived in a large cooperative household, suddenly had an unexpected household meeting to deal with, so there was timing to figure out—there was no point in Jacobine arriving until after the meeting. To be sure, every time Jacobine was in town, Julia's schedule was dense-packed and it was always a logistical feat to spend time together, although normally they succeeded in having at least one dinner or overnight.

After spending the night at Julia's, then catching up on email and such at a café, she met Penny for lunch before going over to SF MoMA, where there proved to be a Robert Rauschenberg show. Jacobine had never been deeply interested in Rauschenberg or other artists of his generation, preferring the socially conscious artists of the 1930s, but she ventured in and grew excited by what she saw. Texture! Assemblage! Photography! She liked Rauschenberg much more now. She wasn't sure, however, that she was much impressed with recent changes to the building. The "renovation" of SF MoMA, done despite the building's relatively recent construction, had removed the wonderfully majestic staircase near the entrance and instead created a strange empty space with no art. Jacobine granted that the building might be larger than before, but she did not find it more architecturally appealing. And yes, one now got to see whole rooms of Anselm Kiefer and Gerhard Richter, but other than a floor of Germans, was everything American mid-century art? She admired two lovely Morris Louis paintings but saw no Helen Frankenthalers. Really, there were not many women at all on display—there were some Louise Bourgeois spiders, but although Jacobine liked Louise Bourgeois, the spiders were by no means her favorites among Bourgeois's works. Ah well. She would need to report back to Kerry about all of this. Meanwhile, as San Francisco had always been a major immigration point, especially for the Chinese and Japanese, there was work she could do in libraries and archives. Immigration from Asia was not her major research focus, but all the same it was part of her overall work, and it might be interesting at some point to put together an exhibition about Chinese settlement in the US and how very few Chinese women were able to come to the country, especially after the Page Act of 1875 had restricted female Chinese immigration in an attempt to clamp down on prostitution, followed by the 1882 Chinese Exclusion Act, which halted Chinese immigration entirely until its repeal in 1943. The Midwest was not a major area of Chinese settlement, but that might be a good reason to do an exhibition on it, rather than a reason not to; not everything had to be about Midwestern topics, although she did like to tie the majority of the shows to the Midwest in some way, even if that way was very tenuous.

52

While still in the Bay Area, Jacobine learned that her aunt Marion had suffered a stroke and died after several days in the hospital. It was unclear whether there would be an immediate funeral or a less immediate memorial; Jacobine's relatives had gone both ways in the past. She supposed that either way the event would be in Las Vegas, where Marion and her family had lived for decades, as Marion had been opposed, in a general way, to returns to the family's origins in northern Wisconsin.

Jacobine supposed that if need be she could get to a funeral over the weekend, although it would almost certainly mean canceling seeing a group of old friends on Saturday. But better this weekend than the next. A later memorial would be even better, but of course her own preferences were hardly what mattered here.

She didn't feel precisely sad at Marion's death—she hadn't known her aunt that well, especially during her adult life. She recalled Marion clearly, and was fond of her, but felt more sorry than truly sad; it hadn't been that likely that they would see each other again, and all that.

• • •

Penny, with whom Jacobine was now staying, mentioned that her own aunt was dying.

"I think tomorrow I'll go to Sacramento to see her before the end," said Penny. "My family usually gathers round at times like this, when someone's near the end and kind of slowly drifting off. It may get kind of strange, because not all of the siblings who are left are exactly in their right minds anymore, but I feel like I should go."

Due to the uncertainty about whether Marion's funeral would be right away, Jacobine hadn't ended up planning anything for the next day apart from tentative plans for supper with Ramon and Nola in the evening, so she wandered about taking pictures in San Francisco for a while and then took BART over to Berkeley to do some library research.

And also, Jacobine noted, between Penny's busy work schedule and the vigil at her dying aunt's in Sacramento, the apartment had begun to go somewhat out of control; Penny hadn't done any laundry in a while and was behind on cleaning and groceries. Jacobine was planning to pick up some groceries, but didn't know just what Penny typically needed these days, which reminded her that *guests and fish stink after three days.*

53

The funerary rites for Jacobine's aunt were at last scheduled and she flew to Las Vegas.

Few relatives came to Marion's memorial. Not embarrassingly few, but not as many as Jacobine would have expected. She wondered whether not enough word had gone out about it—she'd posted the details on Facebook once she had them, but that was no guarantee of anyone seeing. None of the Las Vegas relatives were on Facebook; they didn't stay in touch with the rest of the family except for Christmas cards. They were somewhat cut off from the rest of the clan. Larry was the only one who ever came to any family event outside Las Vegas, and that only rarely.

A few people drove in from their winter homes in Arizona; two other cousins flew. Jacobine's mother initially said she'd go, then decided she couldn't handle flying as her knee was bothering her a lot lately. Jacobine's aunt Letty wasn't up to flying either, so her son stayed home with her; Uncle George and his wife were likewise not in shape to travel; nobody from Aunt Pam's family came, which was surprising, as Karen usually represented them at funerals. Marion's children all came, but Jacobine didn't learn whether all of their children and grandchildren were there. It wasn't clear whether anyone from Marion's husband's family came; maybe by now they had all died, as his family had been small. Marion's church friends came, fortunately, so the pews weren't too empty.

The church was located in a strip mall but was not too bad apart from that and the acoustic-tile ceiling. It was certainly less ugly than the church Marion had taken the relatives to after her husband's cremation. A sign on the door proclaimed this church to be Missouri Synod; Jacobine didn't think she had ever been in a Missouri Synod church unless Marion's previous Las Vegas churches were also Missouri Synod; all the Lutherans in the family had been ELCA as far as she knew. But maybe Las Vegas didn't have many ELCA churches. Or maybe Marion hadn't approved of ELCA's relatively liberal version of Lutheranism; while Jacobine was sure that Marion would have supported women's right to join the clergy, which Missouri Synod did not, it was possible that Marion had opposed same-sex marriage.

As it was Missouri Synod, many things were different than she was used to. The pastor wore flowing vestments, and Jacobine had to fight the urge to photograph him during the service. He was an older man in a cassock and lacy white surplice, with a Lenten purple damask stole bedizened with gold embroidered Chi-Rho symbols above silky fringes. His style of preaching was vocally unremarkable, but he gestured well, more theatrically than she recalled of ELCA pastors.

The hymnal provided an entire section of funeral service for everyone to follow; it appeared that in the Missouri Synod very little was optional, mainly some hymns and bits of sermon. Since the pastor had actually known Marion, although not very well as she had only been at his church for a few years, he had chosen hymns that she had particularly liked. And, as Marion had been a fine singer, Jacobine found them better than most hymns.

But as the pastor had only known Marion for a few years, he had learned only after her death just how deeply involved she had been in church work. This reminded Jacobine of the funeral for another of her aunts, where even though Louise had been a member of the congregation for well over sixty years, the pastor conducting the funeral had arrived too late to experience her constant involvement in everything the church ever did.

Marion's pastor was interested to learn of her deep involvement with charitable works, and said nice things about that, but then undercut it by focusing his sermon on how the way to heaven is through faith alone rather than good works. Jacobine and some of her cousins were annoyed by that, as it was not as if Marion had thought that good works were her ticket to heaven. *Whatever one might think about religion,* thought Jacobine, *there was no question that Marion's faith was central to her life.*

And then, unlike other recent funerals in the family, there was no part of the service for any family member or friend to speak. There was an opportunity afterward at the luncheon, but only two of Marion's children spoke and not enough time was left for the rest of the group to collect their thoughts and volunteer.

The next morning, Jacobine went by herself to the Las Vegas March for Our Lives. It was a big rally—not as big as the marches occurring simultaneously in DC or several other cities—but it was still quite large. After all, there had been the major mass shooting in Las Vegas the previous fall and survivors were available to speak. There were, in fact, quite a few people speaking, and Jacobine found herself positioned so that she could simultaneously see them pretty well on the Jumbotron and distantly in person. It was all very well organized and heartfelt. To be sure, more non-marchers would have *seen* it had the march taken place on the Strip, but it was by City Hall instead, which made sense in a different way.

Jacobine supposed that the smart choice afterwards would have been to get lunch nearby and spend a while photographing around the Arts District—small buildings which looked like what she recalled of Las Vegas from years before, done over with colorful paint—but she figured that as she was in town for family reasons, she should see what family was up to. Most of Marion's immediate family had decamped right after the funeral luncheon, so Jacobine spent most of the afternoon at a casino where the other out-of-town cousins had found rooms.

Conversation flagged, however, in the dim atmosphere of the casino. Jacobine, who had a rental car, suggested that they could all go for a drive in nature before going to Larry and Elaine's for dinner, but naps and video poker proved a stronger draw, so she instead agreed to meet them at Larry's and drove out to Lake Mead on her own. Not that Lake Mead was exactly her idea of unspoiled nature, but at least it was an easy drive and wasn't a casino. She didn't particularly mind casinos after dark, but during the daytime they disgusted her—the cigarette smoke, the jangling of slot machines, the utter lack of natural light—ugh.

Dinner at Larry and Elaine's proved enjoyable. None of the cousins saw Larry that often, and Elaine, who was his third wife, didn't travel with him, so the family didn't really know her at all. Elaine said she and Larry had met at church; and it appeared that they were still happy together after sixteen years of marriage. Their recently built tract house was pleasant and tasteful, even if Jacobine found their collection of religious statuettes of Jesus and crew a bit strange. But she supposed that the emphasis on visible religion was important in casino-land.

And so a good time was had by all despite much discussion of people's health and very little about Marion or the rest of her family.

But it would be good to get away from Las Vegas. Jacobine had found the city somewhat interesting back in the late sixties and early seventies, mainly because it was so different from everywhere else she knew—a dusty desert town with a strip of neon-lit casinos; and it had seemed relatively ordinary if non-water conserving in the eighties and early 2000s, but by now it had grown into a sprawling metropolis with eight-lane parkways all over, streets that were nearly freeways dividing the residential areas from one another. There was new housing everywhere and she suspected that the modest house where Marion and her family had lived in the sixties was now demolished or slum property.

Jacobine couldn't imagine why people chose to live in Las Vegas. Sure, some people loved the desert, and people like Larry grew up there and so had family ties and friends, while others went there to work, but it was just not that enticing. These days people who wanted to gamble had other options. *It's like visiting someplace in a science fiction story,* thought Jacobine, *like we had colonized Mars and set up a grotesque echo of civilization there.*

And it had been unsettling hearing her cousins talk about being old. It was true that apart from Marion's youngest, Jacobine was the youngest cousin in attendance, but the other cousins at dinner were all under seventy. Larry had had two heart attacks but otherwise seemed in good shape; no one else confessed to much more than arthritis.

• • •

At the airport, with time to kill before her flight, Jacobine's attention was drawn to two women around her own age or perhaps slightly older, seated at the next restaurant table. The one nearest her was a proving to be a monologist—an intelligent enough person, but a definite monologist.

The monologist went over how she'd gone to the Sistine Chapel, and also how much she liked Dutch art; how she'd like to go back to Japan someday; how her father had shaved two years off his age to join the Marines in World War II; and how somebody known to both women was an alcoholic artist.

The other woman periodically commented or asked a question, but apparently had nothing in particular to contribute, although the monologist did provide her with occasional openings.

Jacobine was intrigued yet rather annoyed by this conversation. Like Cinda, the one woman clearly felt that she (or at least someone) had to talk ceaselessly, and she was proving to be one of those people who make blanket assessments about people and life in entire countries, as if by visiting Holland or Japan she actually knew how everyone in those places thought or liked to live. *People who sound fairly intelligent tend to get away with that kind of thing,* thought Jacobine. *To those with less experience, they sound amazingly knowledgeable, rather than somewhat shallow.*

"I used to hire a limo to take my kids to the airport," the woman now said, "but things aren't safe in this day and age like when we were kids, when you could leave your door unlocked."

How this related to hiring a limo to take her kids to the airport remained unclear to Jacobine.

"The school shootings began when my son was in high school, and I can't imagine what it must be like now, worrying every time your kid goes to school." She continued to develop this theme for a while, and her companion made suitable noises. Jacobine's attention drifted. She had thought enough about mass shootings for one weekend.

"I used to just love flourless chocolate cake," said the woman next. What the transition had been from school shootings and child safety, Jacobine could not imagine. "I used to bake flourless chocolate cake a lot, especially at Christmas. Flourless chocolate cake, and sugar cookies, and fruit cake..." She went on from there.

Yep, thought Jacobine, *she's just like Cinda, just hopping onto any old topic to make sure there isn't a silence of more than ten seconds.*

"I really enjoyed the conference," said the woman after perhaps exhausting the topic of her Christmas baking.

"Yes, so did I," said her companion. "I wish I could deduct this meal, but I can't because I'm no longer on 'conference time.'"

"That's too bad," said the talker.

Jacobine wondered what their conference had been about. It wasn't clear from their conversation, although the one woman had had a lot to say about art earlier.

However, now the monologist moved on to talking about the warranties on her tires. And, that evidently being a completely unproductive topic, then it was on to how Baja was getting "infested." "But," she observed, "I like the Mexicans, because they're simple people with strong family values, like the Italians and Spaniards."

Jacobine wanted to throw something. How could you possibly generalize about people in such an arrogant, idiotic way?

For a moment it looked as if the women were getting ready to move on, but then they seemed to settle right back down.

"Ellen Greenspan really lasted a lot longer than she should have," said the talker.

"She really suffered," agreed the other.

"These days, though, there's an antibiotic that can target the lower gut and make a person feel so much better." The talker began to dig in her luggage, saying "I hope I didn't lose it!" several times as she piled more and more of the contents of her purse and carry-on onto the chair beside her.

Jacobine watched with furtive fascination—after all, it was impossible to concentrate on her book while this was going on at the next table—

"What're you looking for?" the friend wanted to know.

"I'm looking for a small notebook," was the reply. But why the woman had suddenly wanted to find her notebook remained a mystery, because she began to talk about a movie she had seen about a reincarnated dog, while she continued to dig through her suitcase, incidentally blocking Jacobine's exit, so that it was fortunate Jacobine didn't have to race off just yet. The woman still hadn't found the notebook by the time she finished telling the story of the reincarnated-dog movie, making Jacobine feel almost as though she were watching the reincarnated dog digging through the suitcase.

At last the woman brought forth a small notebook, a fattish spiral-bound item. "Success!" she exclaimed. "Here it is! I really thought I must have lost it somewhere."

Well, thought Jacobine, *I would not pack it in the depths of that suitcase if I were her, I would keep it where I could get at it.* Jacobine believed in being able to take a note at a moment's notice, while the thought was fresh.

This little adventure completed, the two women soon paid their bill and departed, as did Jacobine.

When Jacobine reached the seating area for her return flight, she became aware of an emergency near her gate—a strangely silent one, whatever it was. An elderly woman, or at least one clearly older than Jacobine, was sitting on the floor looking as if she had collapsed there. The medical kit took forever to arrive, and then other passengers kept stepping around and over the poor woman, like idiots. Some people were being helpful, but most were not. Then—additional minutes later—the medics arrived.

Jacobine hoped it would turn out that the woman had merely fainted rather than having a heart attack or some such thing, but then she noticed that there was blood all over the woman's shoulder. Why would there be blood? A bad nosebleed, perhaps? What would cause such a thing? Jacobine couldn't see any blood on the woman's face or head, but then she was some ten feet away in the crowded gate area. It wasn't easy to see exactly what was going on, especially with passengers walking so close to the woman. And then, when boarding began and she proffered her boarding pass to the staff, she didn't suppose she'd ever learn what became of that unfortunate woman at the gate.

54

Trump had said the new tax bill would be "really, really special." As Jacobine prepared her taxes, she was inclined to agree that it was "special," all right. Starting in 2019, the tax rate for big businesses would fall from thirty-five percent to twenty percent. The top tax rate for millionaires would also fall. The wealthy, lucky beasts, would get to keep deducting their contributions to charity, and even fewer of them would have to pay estate tax on inheritance. The less wealthy were supposedly getting a tax cut for the next few years (but only till 2026), but not necessarily, because so many of the tax credits popular with ordinary tax payers had been axed. As the *Washington Post* had pointed out months earlier, "Goodbye to the ability to deduct losses from 'fire, storm, shipwreck, or other casualty, or from theft.' Goodbye to the deduction for tax preparation expenses. Goodbye to the deduction for people who bike to work. Goodbye to the deduction for moving expenses."

And furthermore, the Tax Cut and Jobs Act was more than just a tax bill. It repealed the individual health insurance mandate, meaning that Americans would no longer be required to pay a penalty if they hadn't obtained health insurance. The Congressional Budget Office estimated that this would cause health insurance premiums to rise drastically, thereby prompting millions of people to drop their insurance, which would make premiums go up further for those who remained.

Oh, and the Act also opened up more land in Alaska to oil drilling. *Yeah, that was all pretty special,* thought Jacobine as she noted that her 2018 tax bill would rise as she would no longer be able to deduct unreimbursed business expenses such as travel for research and conferences.

●   ●   ●

One afternoon during tax season, then, as Jacobine arose from her armchair to check the Caller ID on the latest robocaller, she felt a sudden flare of pain in her pelvis. It felt, to be precise, as if her femur was grinding directly against the acetabulum of her pelvis, without the benefit of any cartilage or synovial fluid whatsoever in the joint. While she had been aware for some years that she was developing arthritis, thus far this had confined itself to giving her an occasional stiff back, so she now wondered whether she had pinched a nerve. What if this was sciatica, which her mother had assured her was dreadfully painful? She lurched slowly and carefully forward, no longer even slightly interested in reaching the telephone (and after all the whole idea of getting up to look at the Caller ID was less about identifying callers than about making sure she didn't sit too long at one stretch).

The pain continued; it didn't remain exactly the same sort of pain, but mutated from day to day, sometimes manifesting as a pain in the groin, other times as a tenderness on the side of her hip, and still other times as an ache throughout her thigh. Some days it made walking painful and insecure; some nights the aching kept her awake.

●   ●   ●

On the bright side (so to speak), solar power had overtaken gas and wind as the biggest source of new power in the US. Despite Trump's new tariffs on imported panels, the US was going gangbusters on solar installations. First quarter installations were up thirteen percent from a year earlier, accounting for fifty-five percent of all new generation. Was it, Jacobine wondered, finally time to get solar panels onto her roof? Or was Trump going to slap such heavy tariffs on them that they'd be out of reach for the average householder, and only affordable if you were installing in bulk?

Trump's advisor Mike Pompeo, meanwhile, began negotiations with Kim Jong Un.

55

For quite some time now, Central Americans fleeing hardship and violence at home had been journeying through Mexico and attempting to gain refuge in the US. Whether singly, with friends, or as families, they ventured toward the border. In May, however, Attorney General Sessions announced that anyone entering the US illegally would be charged with a crime. Seeking asylum was not a crime, but crossing the border to request it now became much trickier. Furthermore, since legally the federal government was required to hold children in the least restrictive setting possible, the administration claimed that children could not be imprisoned with their parents. And so began massive family separations and incarcerations.

It was true that during the Obama administration, unaccompanied immigrant children arriving at the border had begun to be temporarily housed in makeshift chain-link enclosures, which had caused an outcry. Under the Trump administration, however, the children in the pens were now largely children forcibly separated from their parents at the border, including babies and toddlers.

In June, the Associated Press reported: "Inside an old warehouse in South Texas, hundreds of children wait in a series of cages created by metal fencing. One cage had 20 children inside. Scattered about are bottles of water, bags of chips and large foil sheets intended to serve as blankets." Strange disputes promptly erupted over whether it was accurate to term chain-link fenced enclosures "cages." The Border Patrol, for example, objected because they were "very uncomfortable" with the implication that they were treating children as animals, and Homeland Security Secretary Kristjen Nielsen pretended that there was no policy of separating families at the border—although it was obviously happening, and at large scale.

The situation rapidly worsened as more and more children were taken from their families, and it was anticipated that as many as thirty thousand of these children might be incarcerated by August. Older children found themselves changing babies' diapers in the absence of adults, and not all of the Indigenous children spoke any Spanish, let alone English. Adults, meanwhile, often had no idea where their children had been taken. Children were to be transferred from immigration detention to the Office of Refugee Resettlement within three days, where they would be placed in ORR shelters previously not mostly intended for very young children, or alternatively they might be put in newly organized tent camps. ORR was then supposed to find family members, foster parents, or sponsors to take the children—preferably parents, to be sure, but as parents who remained in detention could not have their children back, long-term separations began to be commonplace. And it soon became clear that there was no formal protocol for keeping track of either parents or children, and that this inadequate recordkeeping obscured even where a child might be housed.

The shock and outrage felt around the world at needlessly traumatizing so many children—and indeed parents—was compounded when migrant Central American children began to die in federal custody in

December and later when reports of abuse and sexual molestation of migrant children began to multiply.

Jacobine, despite her professional interest in the immigrant experience, could not bear to think of researching the present situation for scholarly publication, and instead sent donations to child welfare organizations and immigrant rights activist groups.

56

In June, possibly as a distraction from caged children, Trump met the North Korean dictator in Singapore, claiming that real estate development, not nuclear weapons, offered the most promising future. North Korea's beachfront real estate could become the site of "the best hotels in the world." During the encounter, Trump showed Kim Jong Un a bizarre four-minute fake movie trailer intended to persuade the dictator to abandon nuclear weaponry; the *Los Angeles Times* described the White House production as looking "like a cross between a propaganda film and movie trailer about an action hero." Or, as the satirist for Britain's *Globe and Mail* put it, "blending sharp and crisp stock footage of what exactly makes America and North Korea so super-fun ... A Story of Opportunity for North Korea is *coming soon to a theatre of war near you.*"

• • •

On Friday, July 13th, the Justice Department indicted twelve Russian intelligence officers for allegedly conspiring to hack the Democrats in 2016. On Monday the 16th, Trump continued, as per usual, to astound and appall the world. Following his controversial visit to the UK, where the British public had vigorously protested his visit well before he insulted, separately and differently, the Queen and the Prime Minister; and where he had told the Prime Minister to "sue" the European Union rather than negotiate over Brexit, then also told CBS news that the European Union was his "biggest foe globally right now," Trump went on to Finland to meet privately with Vladimir Putin. There, he announced that Putin had given him an "extremely strong and powerful" denial that Russia had attacked American democracy, calling the federal investigation of Russian interference "a disaster for our country" and "a total witch hunt," and utterly rejecting the US intelligence agencies' shared conclusion that Russia had indeed interfered in the presidential election. With Putin at his side, Trump insisted that there had been no collusion between his campaign and the Russians, and went on to ramble about his personal grievances and his pet unsubstantiated conspiracy theories.

In response, the Director of National Intelligence stated that the intelligence assessment of Russia's "ongoing, pervasive efforts to undermine our democracy" was clear and had been presented to Trump in an objective fashion. A former CIA director similarly tweeted that Trump had shown himself to be "wholly in the pocket of Putin" and that his remarks were "nothing short of treasonous."

Contemplating Trump's latest antics, Jacobine supposed that in this mysterious private meeting, Trump had probably offered to give Putin Alaska or a prime selection of NATO military bases. She thought, *We must vote out his enablers in November. I need to volunteer to do voter registration.*

• • •

And then, within hours, Maria Butina, a young Russian who had recently received a graduate degree from

American University, was arrested and ordered held without bond, charged with conspiracy to act as an agent of the Russian Federation and accused of trying to cultivate relationships with American politicians and seeking to infiltrate US political groups to advance Russia's agenda. In an affidavit filed with the court, the FBI outlined Butina's alleged two-year effort to penetrate and influence the US political system for Russia's benefit by building ties to the leadership of the National Rifle Association and other right-wing political organizations. While the case was not part of the special counsel investigation into Russian interference, it showed new evidence of Russia's attempts to influence the United States.

Indeed, Butina had been among the various Russians who had attended Trump's inauguration and toasted to better relations between Russia and the United States.

57

Jacobine was feeling quite unhappy with her body's apparent impending disintegration. While her hip and leg had been troublesome throughout the late spring, the various pains largely subsided during June and the first part of July, when she had been doing some traveling and a good deal of walking. But as soon as she returned home, the pains returned too, so she went to the doctor at last and was referred for X-rays and physical therapy. Meanwhile, the pain often kept her awake at night, prevented her from moving the leg very far to the side, and in general made itself troublesome. Although she was still able to walk and ride a bike, the intermittent and extremely varied nature of the pains nonetheless made her feel like an invalid.

Therefore, Jacobine was rather excited about going to her first physical therapy appointment. While she hadn't heard anything yet about the results of her pelvic X-rays, the therapist proved to have access to them, and said they showed arthritis. Strangely, the right side was in worse condition than the painful left side. Jacobine recalled that her father too had found that his painful side wasn't as severely affected as the other side. However, he'd been over eighty at the time, whereas Jacobine was not yet even out of her fifties. She hoped she was not gearing up for early hip replacement. This was not something she brought up, as the therapist was hardly an expert on surgical remedies.

The therapist measured her range of movement in different directions, pulled and pressed different areas, and so on.

"Your leg muscles are weak," concluded the therapist, "and the left leg is weaker than your right leg, plus your hamstrings are very tight, which isn't a good thing. I'll be showing you some stretching exercises that you should begin doing every day."

"Should I sign up for any particular gym classes at school?" asked Jacobine. "I've taken fencing in the past, but I suppose that might be too strenuous right now."

"Right now you should just concentrate on your therapy, but later on you might try something like tai chi or possibly yoga."

The therapist explained that the random nature of the pain was actually typical of arthritis—the pelvis referred pain to the leg, so the pelvis was to blame for thigh pains and even the occasional calf pains. The important thing was to do lots of stretches and gentle exercise, because when it came to arthritis, resting was not going to help, but would simply make matters worse.

Overall, Jacobine was very pleased with the therapist.

• • •

At work, meanwhile, Jacobine found herself lamenting that although computers had made numerous tasks easier or even simply possible, they also ate up maddening amounts of time with their irritating technical glitches. And that wasn't counting all the time she was spending lately deleting hundreds of emails; she received so many political emails that each day Gmail displayed a new message warning her that it was nearly out of space. Once politicians and charities had discovered the power of email, they took to bombarding the world with spam, meaning that the recipients read almost none of their messages, especially those with subject lines like "All is lost" and "Hey!"

In the course of a major email deletion binge, therefore, Jacobine was not terribly surprised to discover, in her spam folder, a blackmail threat asserting that if she didn't pay up, the sender would make public a trove of captured masturbatory porn featuring her. It was nasty—she had no doubt that some recipients would freak out and pay— and it was cleverer than the standard Nigerian scam emails that tended to greet one as "Dearly Beloved," as this email inserted her name into the text. But of course mail-merge software had been able to do *that* for decades, it was just a bit disturbing that this particular form had both the email address and the name that went with it, suggesting that this demand was the result of one of those big hack jobs carried out upon major banks, insurers, and so on, perhaps by a Russian troll farm.

Jacobine was tempted to respond with a jeering email but restrained herself. Still, she thought, it would be pretty cool if someone programmed a way to flood the blackmailer's system with millions of insults, or with ten-megabyte dick photos or something like that. Even if these blackmailers had actually somehow obtained racy photos of her from a past paramour, there would be no real cause for alarm, as after all one could Photoshop anyone's head onto anyone else's body. She'd say publish and be damned. But the existing racy photos of her were, she thought, pretty tame stuff by blackmail standards, and she doubted that any of them were in the hands of blackmailers.

"I am sure people are more interested," she told a colleague, "in the current idiocy in which a perhaps not so bright Democratic candidate has accused her Republican opponent of being into Bigfoot porn. Why she cares about a silly picture of the censored drawing of Bigfoot when her opponent has ties to white supremacists is my question."

"Bigfoot porn is funnier," said her colleague.

"Yes, but let's keep white supremacists out of office, please!"

"Quite," said her colleague.

"Well, and as if Bigfoot porn weren't enough, there is also the white-supremacist Republican idiot politician that Sacha Baron Cohen duped into capering about bare-assed yelling 'America' and pretending to be Chinese. When you have that kind of insanity in the news, or for that matter the daily horrors of the Trump administration, the idea that anyone imagines they can extort money out of me with threats of exposing my home sex life—nonexistent as it currently is—is just quaint."

58

In early August, Jacobine went to see Cinda, who was now full of ideas about moving to Santa Fe.

"I'm still dithering about where I ought to live when I retire," said Cinda. "Whatever happened with that lovely house I looked at in your neighborhood? Is it still for sale, by any chance?"

"You looked at it over a year ago, so of course it's no longer for sale," said Jacobine. "As a matter of fact, I asked my neighbor about it, and he said it was already sold when you saw it. I suppose it was in escrow then or something."

"That can't be right," said Cinda. "I'm sure he told me it was for sale."

"Well, I don't know what he told you, but it's not for sale anymore. Houses in my neighborhood tend to sell in a matter of days now. It's crazy."

"I'm applying for some interesting jobs in Santa Fe," said Cinda. "Their online application portal is a disaster, though! I simply could not figure it out. I'm not even sure whether my completed applications are properly submitted!"

"Surely there's some way you can tell if everything is submitted," said Jacobine.

"Well, that's part of the problem!" said Cinda. "I can't tell."

"Then I would suspect your applications aren't in."

"I hate online job applications," said Cinda. "You'd think that by this time people would know how to design them, but so often they're absolutely byzantine. Anyway, in the meantime I've been looking at real estate options in Santa Fe, and once again prices are simply through the roof. I specified a range that I was willing to look at, and there was almost nothing available. But I did see one possible house in my price range, a little adobe with a big enough yard, and it's really cute." She proceeded to describe the adobe in considerable detail, along with its location and current ownership. "There is some kind of problem with easements, and the house would need some renovations, but I'm really tempted. I might go ahead and buy it even if I don't get one of these jobs."

"Can you afford to do that?"

"Well, I'd need to do some maneuvering," said Cinda. "I have a little more than a year before I turn sixty-five, so there's the question of whether I should try to stick it out at the museum here until then."

"So... what exactly would you do?" Jacobine could never quite make sense of Cinda's financial and retirement planning—she didn't know what was reasonable for a person in Cinda's particular situation to do.

"Well, obviously if I got one of the Santa Fe jobs, I'd buy the adobe, sell the house here, and move to Santa Fe. But if I bought the adobe and didn't get a job in Santa Fe, I'd either be renting it out short-term while I finished up at the museum, or I'd move now and either sell the house here right away or rent it out for a while before selling. It might be a smarter move financially to rent it out, but on the other hand it's not that easy to handle a long-distance rental property. I'd really need to have a property manager, and that might not be worth the expense."

"If you didn't get whatever you applied for in Santa Fe, would you just retire early then if you left the museum, or would you find some other kind of job?" inquired Jacobine. She couldn't remember whether Cinda would get any pensions from previous jobs, or if she had annuities, or whether Cinda still had any of the money she'd inherited or whether Cinda's family had ended up selling the riverfront property out west. Cinda would get Social Security, of course, but could she wait till sixty-five or seventy to begin taking it? The longer you waited, the larger the monthly payment.

"Oh, I'd need to find some sort of part-time work," said Cinda. "Something to supplement my Social Security without replacing it."

"What do you suppose you'd do?"

"I've got various possibilities in mind," said Cinda. "For instance, I might start a dog-walking business. And I could teach yoga classes. I have some other thoughts as well, but whatever I did would need to be flexible so that I could travel. Santa Fe provides good access for quite a bit of regional outdoor activity, but I also want to do as much international travel as I can while I'm still able. After all, I haven't been to Machu Picchu yet, and I'd really like to go to Iceland. I'll need to do some of the more physically demanding travel while my body can still handle it."

As usual, Cinda rambled on endlessly about dogs. Some of it was reasonably interesting—Jacobine gradually concluded that Cinda must be working with rescue dogs on a fairly serious basis, and she finally figured out that "my rep," whom Cinda kept mentioning, must be someone in whatever rescue organization she was dealing with. This was much more interesting to Jacobine than Cinda's repeated accounts of how she'd almost broken various lamps and vases by throwing balls in the house for the new dog, or her references to a foster dog who kept "proving his breed" by sitting on the table.

59

At Jacobine's next physical therapy appointment, she learned that she'd been able to regain some range of movement just in the past week. That was definitely a relief; while the arthritis might be causing some pain, perhaps most of her trouble was actually from tightness in her leg muscles and hamstrings. Increased attention to doing all of her twice-a-day exercises sounded key. Maybe soon she'd even be able to spread her legs normally again—because how would she ever have sex again if she couldn't part her legs to any extent?

Still, now that she was fifty-nine, she wasn't too happy to be just one year from sixty; sixty still marked the beginning of old age even though vigorous health had become common for people in their sixties. And, for the most part, she remained vigorous—but this damned arthritis threatened to be very troublesome. Even if she got her muscles and tendons back in shape, how much could be done about the actual arthritis and the pain in the pelvis that often stabbed her when she walked these days?

• • •

Upon learning of Jacobine's arthritis, her mother, who liked to recount all of the exercises she did each day, now informed Jacobine that it would be wise to lose some weight "because excess weight is hard on the knees."

"About the only time I ever *lose* weight anymore is when I'm sick," replied Jacobine, whose weight was actually quite reasonable for her age. "Since I already eat a moderate, healthy diet, I'd really have to exercise a *lot* more in order to lose much weight."

"You're not as heavy now as you were for a while," her mother conceded.

Jacobine had indeed gained some weight after beginning her job, and in the last few years had gradually lost some of it again. But did her mother imagine that people needed to be told when they gained weight? If she were truly fat, it would be just cruel to be told she should lose weight. So many people had real trouble with their weight in ways Jacobine did not, and they couldn't simply decide, as Jacobine periodically did, that they wouldn't have any rice with their greens at supper for a while. Jacobine didn't enjoy most of the popular fattening foods, and she wasn't inclined to eat when stressed or unhappy, but rather tended to lose her appetite.

Now, on the whole Jacobine's mother was pleasant and reasonably tactful, and did not frequently make remarks on Jacobine's appearance, but like most mothers, she did feel—and always had—that it was part of her maternal duty to tell her daughter which aspects of her appearance needed improvement. And so, just before saying goodbye, she felt obliged to remind Jacobine, who had long dyed her hair a deep van dyke brown, just this side of black, "You know, I still prefer your hair brown."

When Jacobine mentioned this comment to Nathan, he inquired "What kind of brown is she talking about?"

"A muddy medium brown."

"And when was your hair last a muddy medium brown?"

To which Jacobine said "Only forty-one years ago."

60

Senator John McCain finally, after an impressive struggle to remain politically active, succumbed to his brain cancer, which temporarily distracted the public from North Korea, the Mueller investigation, caged migrant children, and the Black Lives Matter and #MeToo movements, not to mention the storms surrounding Trump's nomination of Brett Kavanaugh for the Supreme Court. Yet Jacobine was unpleasantly aware of how much downtime she seemed to need and how while she didn't watch TV, she did spend time doing things like reading not-so-vital news stories. Did she really need to know what everyone said in their online eulogies of Senator McCain?

So many people saw John McCain as a hero. At another time in history, she thought, he wouldn't have seemed very heroic, just a standard-issue politician who made some good and some bad choices and could apologize for some of the bad ones. These days, though, the rest of the Republicans were in such lockstep with Trump that McCain shone in comparison. It was true he had been a prisoner of war and survived torture, and Jacobine respected him for that. She couldn't assume that she herself would have any been braver than he was when he signed his confession after torture, and she took no position on whether being tortured as a POW made one a war hero or not. His occasional refusals to go along with Trump did not strike her as all that brave. But the other

Republicans, who couldn't tear themselves away from supporting Trump, were in her view a worthless pack of traitors.

And then the Trump White House seemed to be getting ready to implode, with the publication in the *New York Times* of an anonymous op-ed by someone claiming to be part of the White House "resistance." So was this a good thing or was an inside coup underway?

Trump was, inevitably, going bonkers over the anonymous op-ed while his staff was busy denying writing it yet not denying any of its allegations. If staff was having to prevent Trump from ordering assassinations and suchlike, why was he not being bodily removed under the Twenty-fifth Amendment?

61

September neared its end, and Hurricane Florence was due to reach North Carolina.

At the neighborhood social, Cathy Clark said "Davy and I just got back from North Carolina—luckily we got away before any weather hit."

"Climate change certainly seems to be resulting in a lot more hurricanes," said Suzanne DuPre.

"I know," said Cathy. "Harvey and Irma and Maria last year and now Florence!"

Suzanne commented, "I've heard reports that many of the injuries happen because people go outside to see the storm and then get hit by flying metal."

"I've heard that too," said Jacobine. "I wouldn't have thought of it, but once I heard about it, it seemed kind of obvious."

Davy Clark then returned to their table with a second plate of food and began boasting about how many hurricanes he had experienced. "I've stood outside watching lots of them," he claimed. "They're usually no big deal."

Suzanne pointed out, again, "Apparently a lot of the injuries occur when people go outdoors to watch."

"Aw, the media just loves to exaggerate how bad the weather is," said Davy.

"Sure, they're going to focus on where it's worst," said Jacobine, "but I heard about the injuries from a doctor who was interviewed on NPR. He'd had to treat a lot of wounds people suffered from flying debris during the high winds."

"I hope Florence doesn't turn out to be as bad as Maria," said Suzanne.

"It sounds like Puerto Rico was absolutely devastated," said Jacobine. "Two major hurricanes in a row. I can't believe that the death toll there can possibly be as low as it's reported."

"No," agreed Suzanne, "the official death toll is suspiciously low. With electricity out and communications and roads disrupted for the past year, I don't see how they can have any idea even now."

"Puerto Rico is massively corrupt," asserted Davy. "They don't do anything right. All these claims that Puerto Rico doesn't have any fresh water, for instance. That's just bullshit. I've seen news footage of bottles of water just sitting in a field rotting—it's obvious they don't need more fresh water."

Jacobine and Suzanne exchanged glances.

"Whether Puerto Rico has corrupt or incompetent government is not the point," said Jacobine. "We know that people are suffering and dying. Since when is local corruption a deal-breaker when it's a question of saving the lives of American citizens during a disaster?"

"We've sent plenty of aid," said Davy. "They just wasted it."

For the dessert segment of the social, Jacobine sat with a different group of neighbors, all of whom she happened to know were Democrats. The topic of hurricanes did not resurface. Instead, Bob Donald—a nice and intelligent man, but going a little senile—rambled on endlessly about tracing his ancestors twenty generations back and how he had alerted Congress to something or other several decades ago. Jacobine had done enough genealogy to know that it was fairly uncommon to be able to trace a line ten generations, so unless you had royal ancestry, twenty generations were pretty questionable indeed. Even if you had the documentation, you couldn't be sure there weren't "non-paternal events" along the way such as adultery and adoption. She pointed this out, but Bob just wanted to talk about how his family went back to the Plantagenets.

After Florence actually hit, Davy got online announcing which church everyone could send donations to for hurricane relief. *So,* thought Jacobine, *hurricanes are minor nuisances unless his church gets involved.* She did a quick search of past emails to see whether he had called for donations for the previous year's hurricanes. Harvey yes, Irma and Maria no. So hurricanes affecting white people on the mainland were apparently more important than hurricanes affecting Hispanic Americans offshore.

62

One of the neighbors posted an email warning that a car had been stolen. This wasn't exactly a typical crime in Jacobine's neighborhood; usually information about crime related to car and garage break-ins, scrappers who stole copper piping from empty houses, and the heroin addicts from adjoining neighborhoods who bought their drugs on the streets or shot up in the alleys. Usually announcements of bad or sad news got a sympathetic response, but in this case expressions of sympathy for the anonymous theft victim, and for that matter the usual stream of advice about locking doors, were completely pre-empted when Deb Dowd suddenly took the news of the stolen car as an occasion to embark on a tirade about how the neighborhood had become "divisive and dangerous" and "political," and a place where people "hope perilous things happen to others."

Suzanne pointed out, rationally, that "Differing political views don't cause crime."

A couple of others made similarly normal comments. Then Deb began to rave that "our signs were pilfered!" without explaining what sort of signs had disappeared. She went on to rage that a local Democratic candidate had happened to see her and others scraping asphalt from their street, a task which they had undertaken in order to expose the historic brick underneath and which was a new pet project for some residents including the Dowds—but the candidate wouldn't join them because she was on the campaign trail wearing white and couldn't get dirty just then. According to Deb, the Democratic candidate had no understanding of historic districts, and as "the underground political system" was "affecting the crime of the neighborhood," therefore the neighborhood should "leave the politics at the door" and not talk about the upcoming election.

As no one had said a word about politics on the email list for months prior to Deb's rant—politics were, in fact, officially off limits for the neighborhood list and were grounds for being removed from it—Jacobine and other neighbors were startled at this bizarre response to the public service mention of a car theft.

Jacobine usually tried to stay out of strange email exchanges, but in this case she felt obliged to point out that whatever one might think politically, the candidate in question was well known for rehabbing numerous houses in a nearby historic district and therefore the fact that she was unwilling to peel asphalt from Deb's street on a given day had nothing to do with whether she was familiar with historic districts, she was simply not dressed for the job and had other plans for her day. After hitting Send, Jacobine noticed that the list had been asked to abandon the topic, so she felt rather stupid, but no one attacked her online and she wasn't bumped from the list.

A day or so later when she was out for a walk, a neighbor emerged from her house to thank her for her comment.

63

Jacobine had agreed to meet Cinda for a hike with dogs and (of course) Cinda then called to say that her GPS had sent her all over the state. Why Cinda thought she needed GPS to get to a location where they had often hiked in years past, Jacobine could not imagine; it was not a complicated drive from where Cinda lived. Even if the GPS sent her the slow route via country roads, it still wasn't *complicated*. Jacobine groused that people's reliance these days on GPS over a map and common sense was just mindboggling. At this rate, soon no one would have a clue how to figure out a route on their own.

"How are your classes going?" asked Cinda once they were embarked on their path.

"I'm not teaching this semester, it's a museum-only semester," said Jacobine. "The department is actually going to be a little under-staffed next year, what with Beth and Tom getting sabbaticals approved."

"Kerry ought to get a sabbatical, she was hired before they were," asserted Cinda, who was acquainted with most faculty in Kerry and Jacobine's departments.

"Well, yeah, but first Kerry has to apply and the committee has to like her application," said Jacobine. "You know we aren't so lucky as to have automatic sabbaticals every seven years."

"She deserves one!"

"Yes, but I think that right now she's more focused on her teaching. I don't think she's applied. I've suggested she apply for a Fulbright, but I don't think she's applied for that either."

"Well, there's no question she deserves it."

Jacobine did not deny it.

"Would these sabbaticals mean you'd have an opening for me to teach a Museum Studies course or two?"

"That's conceivable," said Jacobine. "I'll ask Mark about it." She knew that this was something Cinda was well qualified to do—Cinda had taught for them in the past—so she was quite willing to promote the idea.

64

Late at night when putting down her book or laptop, Jacobine often found her thoughts rambling over end-of-life topics, which was rather disturbing, considering that people so often did that not long before they actually died. At present, to be sure, she had just learned that her friend Penny's breast cancer, which had been in remission for several years, had returned. Penny was now riddled with it, so could not be expected to live very long.

Jacobine was naturally upset at learning of Penny's impending demise. Nor did she like the way she often lay in bed at night thinking about needing to update her will or wondering why she ever bought new and unnecessary stuff anymore when she had enough belongings and didn't need any more jackets or vases or neat fossils. She didn't like wondering if she'd be one of those countless people who abandoned their deepest dreams and ambitions and simply filled the remaining days with things that didn't matter much, like reading books that she ended up not liking, or looking up when every distant relative's spouse had died so that their birth-marriage-death-burial dates were properly recorded in the family tree.

Reading more of her email, Jacobine learned that an Avaaz activist had donated her lungs when she died, enabling someone else to receive a double lung transplant. She had had no idea that lung transplants were even possible. Who got these transplants? Could Fran have been alive today with a lung transplant? Did you have to have a really close match, as with kidney transplants? To be sure, it mattered how you died, and there wouldn't be much point in transplanting a ninety-year-old organ, or one from someone who had died of cancer. She supposed that organ transplants must come mostly from youngish people who died in the hospital after car accidents.

● ● ●

Meanwhile, Trump praised Kim Jong Un at one of his campaign rallies, claiming that he and the North Korean dictator "fell in love. I was really being tough and so was he," said Trump. "And we would go back and forth. And then we fell in love. No really. He wrote me beautiful letters. They were great letters. And then we fell in love," he continued fatuously as he contemplated a possible second summit with Kim.

65

That fall, Jacobine went to a museum studies conference, rooming for the first time with her friend Liz, who normally roomed with a mutual friend who couldn't attend this time. Liz also worked at a university, in a combined faculty-museum position similar to Jacobine's; and she proved to have an enormous amount to say, as they only saw each other at these conferences, and much had been happening in Liz's life.

Jacobine already knew from past conversations that Liz's university was a fairly poor place to work and that Liz and her husband had divorced, but she had had no idea until now that Liz's school was quite as problematic a workplace as it now sounded. There seemed to be absolutely nothing there that was not dysfunctional and bizarre. To begin with, Liz, who was an art historian, was no longer situated in the Art Department but had moved to a mixed department that included Communication and Anthropology as well as Museum Studies.

"It's just so strange!" exclaimed Liz. "I'm the only art historian on campus, and the art students have to take art history courses, but the artists back in the Art Department hate me—I don't know *why*—and so instead of having their students take my courses, they've created their own *pseudo-art-historical* offerings for majors, which are taught by a woman who used to teach jewelry design but now teaches Art Appreciation along with this really poorly designed course on Japanese art. She doesn't know a thing about Japanese art—I ran the syllabus by some nonwestern specialists and they were just appalled, it was so bad!"

"How is she even allowed to teach this course, if she isn't qualified?" inquired Jacobine, who knew that while an MFA degree was required to teach college-level studio courses, coursework past the MA was required to teach art history beyond the intro level. So this woman needed to have a PhD, or at least be ABD, if this Japanese course was upper-level.

"I don't know," exclaimed Liz, "she's definitely not qualified, so the department will be in big trouble when it's time for them to renew their NASAD accreditation. What's more, she's not mentally stable either. I think part of that is because the rest of the department decided to stop offering jewelry design as a concentration, and that's her area of expertise. She's a tenured professor, so I don't understand why they decided to scrap her concentration. Presumably she wouldn't have gotten tenure if she hadn't been competent in her area of concentration! But that all happened before I was hired, so I'm sure it's been *festering* for a long time."

"Very odd," said Jacobine.

"And things are almost as crazy in my current department!" Liz went on. "For instance, one of my colleagues went into the classroom one day and found *what turned out to be a loaded Glock on the lectern!*"

"*What?*" said Jacobine.

"A loaded Glock!"

"That's absolutely horrifying. How did it get there?"

"Well!" said Liz. "That's where it gets even crazier!"

"Crazier than a Glock on the lectern?"

"Yes! You see, my colleague who *found* the Glock didn't realize at first what it was, because it was in what just seemed like some sort of folder or portfolio, I guess. And so he opened this up to see if there was any identification inside so he could return it to whoever left it there. He wasn't being especially careful handling the folder or carrying case thingy because he had no idea that he was going to find a *Glock* inside!"

"Holy cow," said Jacobine.

"Exactly!" said Liz. "So he opened it up and discovered this Glock! In his classroom! On his lectern! Can you imagine? I mean, he must've practically peed his pants. He could've accidentally set it off opening the folder—what if he'd shot someone? He could've shot himself! My colleague was already having a really difficult semester— he was having a lot of health problems, some of which were actually due to unsafe conditions on campus. *Anyway*, once he saw the *Glock*, he very gingerly picked up the whole thing, the folder or case plus the gun, and took it in to the departmental office to report it and call the campus police."

"Oh my god," said Jacobine. "Then what?"

"You won't believe this, it's so friggin' crazy. It turned out that the *Glock* belonged to *another professor*, who for *some reason* had taken it to class with him and left it behind—*forgot* it—there!"

"That's bizarre beyond words. What was this guy doing bringing a gun to class? And how does anyone forget they've got a Glock along?"

"I don't know *what* he was thinking," said Liz. "He had a concealed carry permit, which is just crazy to begin with if you ask me, but he had *no reason whatsoever* to bring his *gun* into the classroom, especially if he was going to *leave it lying around* and then *forget* it so that anyone could pick it up and *shoot somebody* with it. And then it turned out that he had *a whole arsenal* in his car."

"That is just mind-boggling," said Jacobine.

"He's now been put on administrative leave, at least," said Liz, "but the professor who *found* the gun is traumatized—he can barely spend time in that building anyway because he has a mold allergy and our building is seriously moldy. Well, and the *rest* of us are traumatized too, because who knows what this professor who *brought* the gun was planning to *do* with it? What if they let him come back to school?"

"God," said Jacobine. "Is he young, or fairly close to retirement?"

"I think he's close to retirement, so maybe they'll work out some kind of deal where he just doesn't come back. But really!"

"That sounds like a seriously awful work environment," said Jacobine.

"It's so stressful," said Liz. "That's probably the worst thing, the professor leaving the Glock on the lectern, but it's just *one* incident in an endless parade of crazy and obnoxious and hazardous things that go on at my university."

Liz went on to describe how the colleague who had found the Glock had previously broken his leg descending a steep hill on campus, so that he was on crutches with his leg in a cast when carrying the Glock to the departmental office.

"Our parking situation is just *terrible*," said Liz. "It's a commuter campus, too, which makes things even worse because almost *everybody* is hunting for parking."

"Do you have separate areas for students versus faculty and staff?" asked Jacobine.

"Yes, but that doesn't help at all," said Liz. "None of us can find parking close to where we need to be. So for instance there's a new parking garage that was supposed to be for people in our part of campus, but we can't use it because part of it collapsed. So there is this student parking lot, up a steep hill from our building, where faculty are supposed to park if there aren't any faculty slots open. And because there's no actual proper *path* with *steps* and a *railing* so that people can safely negotiate their way down the hill to our building, that's why my colleague fell and broke his leg."

"Ouch!" exclaimed Jacobine.

"I know," said Liz. "I've fallen on that hill too, but at least I haven't *broken my leg.*"

"Surely your Building and Grounds committee, or OSHA, or somebody, should be doing something about that?"

"Of course they should, but so far they haven't," said Liz. "I can't imagine why. It's a *death trap* and I don't know why the university hasn't been sued yet. And furthermore, faculty shouldn't be directed to park in the student lot anyway."

"No, it's hardly fair to the students to have faculty taking their spaces."

"Not at all," said Liz, "and what's more, they can get really ticked off at us for taking their parking, because the *parking passes* for faculty look *different* from the passes for students, so they can see right away when faculty are parking in their lot. I recently got a really *nasty* note on my car from a student who called me an 'ass-hat' and told me to park in my own lot. As if I wouldn't have parked in my own lot if I *could* have!"

"It's understandable that they're angry, but being rude isn't going to solve anything."

"Exactly, I mean, calling me an *ass-hat!* It's the *university's* fault that I can't park where I'm supposed to, not *my* fault."

"I really don't get why this strange term has become such a popular form of abuse lately," mused Jacobine. "It's not like it's either more acceptable or more disgusting than calling someone an asshole."

"Either way, you can see what a hostile work environment I'm in, with colleagues who bring *Glocks* to school and where students are lashing out at faculty over *parking spots*. At this rate I can't imagine how I'll ever make full professor, either, because the way we do promotions is crazy too."

"You need to find a different job," said Jacobine. "Not that it's easy to do a lateral move as an Associate Professor. But every now and then there are open-rank positions advertised."

"I can't apply for anything very far away," said Liz, "because Joe and I have joint custody of the kids. But since I'm at a state school, in theory I could move to a different state school in the system."

"I think you should try to do that," said Jacobine. "Life is too short to be putting up with what you're describing, if it's at all possible to go somewhere else." She knew that Liz worked extremely hard, teaching a heavy course-load with far more students than the art historians at Jacobine's school, and that in addition to teaching large classes, doing museum work, and having custody of her kids five days a week, Liz presented papers at conferences fairly regularly, published articles now and then, and did staggering amounts of university service. Liz was in fact the ideal poster-girl for the stereotype of the overextended, underappreciated, female Associate Professor.

Liz was also upset with her ex-husband and his arrangements for the kids' activities. Jacobine had barely known him, so she had no particular views about either him or the divorce. However, as Liz and Joe had joint custody of their kids, they had to deal with each other regularly, and consequently Liz had much more to say about him now than she had ever had during their marriage, and none of it was positive. However, while Jacobine had a good opinion of Liz and no real experience with Liz's ex, she was inclined to think that when it came to joint custody, the two just got on each other's nerves. Joe might have many faults, but at least he didn't sound like he was shirking his parental responsibilities. Jacobine refrained, for the present, from offering this potentially irritating assessment.

Both Liz and Jacobine enjoyed the conference, and declared themselves willing to share a hotel room again in the future. A less agreeable outcome of the trip was that Jacobine's cell phone fell out of her bag on the cab ride back to the airport, and although it was labeled with her address and home phone number, the finder did not return it or contact her, but instead somehow succeeded in having the account transferred to him- or herself, as Jacobine discovered when she asked a representative of T-Mobile to investigate why she could not even reach her old number anymore. As the phone was eleven years old, Jacobine was initially mystified that anyone else would want it, but she later learned that old phones like hers were in demand as "burner" phones by crooks—and even just ordinary people—who wanted cheap phones that didn't reveal too much to callers.

Jacobine decided that as she seldom used her cell phone—she mainly used it when traveling—a new phone could wait. The old phone had cost almost nothing in monthly service, as she only paid for what she actually used rather than paying a monthly fee, and she had no particular desire to get a smartphone.

66

Meanwhile, Jacobine's hip had improved as a result of her physical therapy and stretches, but her doctor and the physical therapist had both recommended that she see an orthopedist to learn more about how her condition would develop in the future. The orthopedist's staff took more X-rays—from standing this time—and asked an array of questions. The orthopedist did not spend long with her, but said that while eventually she would need a hip replacement, in the meantime there were numerous ways of alleviating pain and putting off surgery. Jacobine could continue physical therapy, doing exercises and water therapy and such; she could take supplements like turmeric; take painkillers; have cortisone injections; perhaps later receive platelets and stem cells; and generally see what new treatments developed over the years. As time went by, there would be new treatment options, and her insurance might begin to cover options that it didn't currently.

So while it was a brief visit, Jacobine felt she had a good idea of what the overall future looked like for her arthritic hips. It didn't sound pleasant, but neither did it sound dire.

67

But in the world at large, things were less calm and certainly less promising. The murder of journalist Jamal Khashoggi inside the Saudi embassy in Turkey, the sending of pipe bombs to prominent Democrats, and the mass shooting at the Tree of Life synagogue in Pittsburgh's Squirrel Hill district, along with pretty much anything that issued from Donald Trump's mouth or fingers, caused Jacobine to rant and weep.

"I hate living in a fascist state!" she told Kerry. "This madness has to end. We've got to show Trump and his crew that their days in power are numbered!"

"I'm encouraged by the number of exciting new Democratic candidates that are on the ballot for the November election," said Kerry. "Maybe some of them will even be elected."

"I certainly hope so," said Jacobine. "It's not the right time to vote third-party, alas, so I'm voting for any Democrat I can, and for whatever the Sierra Club endorses."

"There are a lot of female candidates this time, and even people of color," said Kerry. "Most of them aren't in our area, but I've sent some of them donations anyway."

"Yes, so have I," said Jacobine. "I like this strategy of spreading many small donations among candidates across the country. Something has to break the influence of the big lobbyists and corporate donors, anyway."

"Especially the influence of the NRA," said Kerry.

"Yes," said Jacobine. "They've abandoned their roots and gone totally wild. I don't see how any reasonable gun owner can see fit to belong to the NRA anymore. Not that I think any reasonable person needs to own a gun, but that's a different matter. Lots of reasonable people do own guns, it's not just all those rabid gun nuts."

•   •   •

And soon there was considerable good news from the midterm election—Democrats retook the House of Representatives—although there was not the extent of "blue wave" that had been hoped for, probably due to Trump rampaging about stirring up his "base" and raving about how the Central Americans fleeing poverty and violence at home would be a huge threat when they (or in other words some small percentage of the migrant "caravan") reached the border.

But although the election news was encouraging, and an exciting roster of new Democrats would be taking office in January, Jacobine still felt she wasted too much time reading the news. Did she *need* to know that the CIA had evidence that the Saudi crown prince had ordered Jamal Khashoggi's murder? Did she *need* to know every new vile thing Trump had said, done, or encouraged? It was important to be an informed citizen, but really, she felt, she could do nothing whatsoever about some of this, nor did most of it relate to her scholarly writing.

And when she thought of the people in her life who were *fortunate* to have died before Trump's election—well—it seemed like her father and various older friends would have gone out of their minds at what went on now. Jacobine supposed her own stress level was actually fairly low compared to that of most people she knew; she really only flipped out late at night while waiting to fall asleep.

68

Thanksgiving with Jacobine's mother and a smattering of other relatives was pleasant enough, but not as interesting as it might have been. Various familiar topics were rehashed by all concerned, with minor updates, but there was little new or remarkable in their family to discuss, meaning that matters relating to health took up much of the conversation. Therefore Jacobine learned that as her mother had recently had her first cataract surgery, Jacobine's aunt Rose, who lived nearby, was engaged in helping her with a course of medicinal eyedrops. They were also waiting for some adjustable reading glasses to arrive in order to see if these would work for Jacobine's mother while she awaited her second cataract surgery and a revised eyeglass prescription—and this purchase of reading glasses was becoming its own little saga as FedEx had gotten the package to Baltimore on Friday morning but then for some reason had handed it off to the postal service instead of delivering it. Jacobine heard a lot from her relatives about the insanity of such a maneuver, although presumably the glasses would arrive on Monday or at the very latest on Tuesday.

And Jacobine wished her mother would go ahead and get a hearing aid, as while her hearing wasn't dreadful, it wasn't great, and apparently if one couldn't hear properly, one actually lost brain function through not having appropriate auditory stimulation, so no wonder her mother didn't seem quite as smart as she used to be. Fortunately, Jacobine's mother did say she had decided to go ahead and get one, just did not want to do so right now when she was dealing with cataract surgeries and removing small skin cancers. Jacobine found this an understandable position.

69

Jacobine had been thinking about contacting Cinda about going ice-skating, as they both enjoyed that in the winter, but Cinda beat her to the punch with an email after Christmas, so Jacobine promptly replied that she was interested. But then there was no response whatsoever. The next day, therefore, Jacobine called and left a message, but again there was no response.

If it had been anyone else, Jacobine would have begun to worry that something had *happened*, like that Cinda had tripped over a dog and fallen and hit her head. But since it was Cinda, she had a hard time thinking it was anything other than Cinda being irritating. Jacobine wished that Cinda had not turned out to be so problematic to hang out with. They did, after all, have so many interests in common, and they could both benefit from having a good friend in the area to do things with. But so many things about Cinda had simply ended up seriously annoying her. Cinda monologued endlessly so that Jacobine usually lost interest in participating in the conversation; she was *always* late; and while her dogs were sweet natured, they were not very pleasant to be around.

Then on Monday morning, the last day of the year, just as Jacobine was contemplating trying to find out if Cinda was all right, Cinda called.

"I can't believe it!" she exclaimed. "I got so wrapped up in repainting my walls that I completely forgot that I'd suggested getting together over the weekend."

"It would have been a great weekend for skating," said Jacobine.

"I know!" said Cinda. "I can't believe I forgot. But I'd bought the paint and it was all pre-stirred and I was so excited about getting it onto the walls before going back to work. By the way, do you know anything about robo-vacuums?"

"Not a whole lot," said Jacobine, "but I did buy one for the living room last year."

"Well, I've been thinking a lot about buying a robo-vacuum," said Cinda, "because I do have quite the ongoing battle with dog hair around here and it's really tiresome to use the big vacuum on it every day. So I'm interested in recommendations."

Jacobine sighed; she was not deeply interested in vacuum cleaners. "They're useful if you don't have too much stuff on the floor like electrical cords and rug fringes. And I like that mine goes most of the way under the couch. Basically I just looked at *Consumer Reports* and ordered the model that they were recommending. They're probably recommending something newer now."

"Do you think a robo-vacuum would be good for dog hair? It's just mindboggling how much the dogs can shed."

"Check *Consumer Reports*," reiterated Jacobine. "You can read it at the library if you don't have a subscription. They always have something to say about which vacuums do well with pet hair."

Cinda conceded that she might be able to pursue this level of product research. "I'd still like to skate," she said next, "but today it's much too rainy to skate outdoors, so what else could we do?"

"Well, what else have you been wanting to do?" said Jacobine, as she knew that Cinda was at least more attuned than she was to various recreational options.

Cinda began to run down a list of December amusements, such as holiday fairs and holiday light displays, but as they gradually looked these up online, most of her suggestions proved to have come to an end over the weekend. Next they began to go through their recollections of favorite restaurants near Cinda's house, with the notion of going out to dinner after engaging in some unspecified afternoon pursuit, but they found that these restaurants had either closed for repairs, gone out of business, or were doing expensive New Year's Eve dinners requiring reservations made weeks in advance.

"That's very disappointing," said Cinda.

"It's not looking promising," agreed Jacobine.

For a moment, it seemed that they might go to a textile exhibition in Cincinnati that both of them had been wanting to see, but then it dawned on them that it was a Monday and so all of the museums were closed.

"Well..." said Cinda. "I had thought the textile show was closing right now, but I see that it's still open next weekend. We could go then... What if we meet for brunch and skating next Saturday and then go to the exhibition?"

"Okay," said Jacobine, eager to get this wrapped up, "so next Saturday we're having brunch, going skating, and then going to this textile exhibition." She wondered, not for the first time, how Cinda ever managed to get anything done, although she knew that of course Cinda did, just as she herself did despite sometimes taking an eternity to plan a simple afternoon's outing.

●　●　●

The next weekend, confident that she and Cinda had a plan for brunch, ice-skating, and textile exhibition, Jacobine decided that as this left the majority of the morning free, she could first go to the farmer's market and then stop briefly at the Container Store and REI on the way to meeting Cinda. But this was not to be.

"Can we change our plans to Sunday?" said Cinda, calling at a startlingly early hour of the morning. "Because..." she switched to a baby-talk voice... "I had a *very exciting day* yesterday." She produced an irritating high-pitched giggle.

"What happened?" asked Jacobine wearily, expecting to learn that Cinda had found the robo-vacuum of her dreams, or some such thing.

But apparently on Friday Cinda had left the dogs at Doggie Day Care only to discover, late in the day, that her latest foster dog had escaped and disappeared in the woods. It was to some extent a replay of an alarming incident of several years earlier when an elderly dog named Ralston had run into the woods during a massive thunderstorm and become trapped under fallen branches—there had been posters and a search party before Ralston was finally rescued—but this time there was a happier ending. Rather than becoming trapped and only being found days later in a debilitated state, the foster dog had emerged on her own late at night and woken the neighbors with her barking. In any case, as this adventure had occupied Cinda until midnight, she felt she was too tired now to do anything but work on her backyard fencing, which needed reinforcement because this same foster dog had been crawling underneath to get into the neighbor's yard.

Jacobine agreed, unenthusiastically, that they could do Sunday instead. She supposed that Cinda would inevitably be late, or cancel again, or whatnot.

On Sunday, Cinda wanted to meet at noon at an outdoor skating rink. Since Jacobine knew from experience that Cinda would be late, she crossed the street to a convenient bookstore and texted suggesting they meet there instead.

Cinda confessed to running late "per usual," saying "glad there is a bookstore."

Did she not know there is a bookstore here? wondered Jacobine. She texted an inquiry as to how late Cinda might be, but as of half past, Cinda had not responded with further details. *This eternal lateness is just so rude,* groused Jacobine to herself. *If we had gotten together yesterday, I could've gone to the Container Store as well as REI, and of course if I didn't have to assume that maybe for once she'd be on time, I could've accomplished something before leaving home, too, rather than spending time hanging around here waiting for her to show up.* While the bookstore was an excellent place to wait around, and she did want to support independent bookstores such as this one, Jacobine nonetheless had several thousand books of her own already and had made it a goal to buy fewer new ones and instead make better use of the library.

Fortunately, once Cinda arrived, they had a largely pleasant time, first having some lunch and then getting in a nice workout at the outdoor skating rink before going to the textile exhibition. It was true, of course, that during lunch almost the entire conversation was about Cinda— and indeed the only thing that wasn't about her was about how perhaps the new gallery coordinator at the university museum wasn't working out. They were fairly far into Jacobine's story about the gallery coordinator before Cinda seemed to realize that Jacobine had exhibited some photographs in a recent faculty show, although it was Jacobine's complaints about her experience that had led to discussion of the gallery coordinator in the first place, so obviously Cinda hadn't been paying attention. But by now Jacobine was pretty much resigned to the fact that Cinda had a limited range of conversational topics, which was to say her dogs, her job, her travel and retirement plans, her outdoor activities, her house and garden, and some art and curatorial topics. She was not likely to talk about anything else unless it had some connection to one of the above topics.

Oh—and yes, there was also Cinda's health as a major topic. During lunch she had told Jacobine all about how she had recently dislocated her hip while dancing, and all about the knee surgery she had had years ago in graduate school and how the knee surgery had revealed that she could never have another surgery on a joint because she belonged to some special percentage of the population that creates massive internal scar tissue. Jacobine found this information fairly gruesome and suspected that hearing it had probably scarred the child seated at the next table for the rest of his life. But she did learn that Cinda had recently enjoyed a trip to Iceland, where she had joined a group climbing on the glaciers there. The Icelandic glaciers were predicted to vanish within the next thirty-five years, so Cinda had been anxious to see them while she could.

The Indian textile show was at the Cincinnati Art Museum, and both Cinda and Jacobine found it to be excellent. It was a show from Britain's V&A, so Jacobine, who had been there not too many years before, thought she recognized some pieces, but most were unfamiliar. Not only were there numerous gorgeous costumes and hangings to look at, but there was much fascinating information about the different types of silkworms bred in India, the types and methods of dye used, the regional fabric-printing techniques and embroidery methods, and so forth.

Altogether, Jacobine thought, this was about as good as an afternoon with Cinda got. Cinda still claimed that Jacobine was the only person she knew who liked to hike, bike, camp, and ice skate, which was hard for Jacobine to believe since most of the time her own engagement in such activities was practically nil. It was true that she enjoyed these activities and wished she could do them more often, but for the most part that desire translated to riding her bike to the farmer's market, the library, and the movie theater on occasions when the weather wasn't too inclement. She supposed that maybe, just maybe, once she retired she could move somewhere conducive to skiing. But chances were poor that she could afford to live anywhere within reach of a ski slope.

70

As January continued, Jacobine again became seriously disturbed by the news from Washington—surely it ought to be illegal for politicians to shut down the federal government! During most of her lifetime, there had never been the slightest thought of "shutting down" the federal government. Prior to 1980, funding gaps had not led to government shutdowns, and shutdowns had not been all that significant until the mid-1990s. More recent shutdowns had caused greater and greater disruption, with a sixteen-day shutdown of all government agencies in 2013, followed by a small three-day shutdown at the beginning of 2018 and now this appalling, seemingly endless, shutdown of 2018–2019, which was caused by disputes over funding Trump's desire to wall off the US from Mexico and which was already becoming the longest shutdown in US history. This latest shutdown, which had cruelly begun just before Christmas, was causing thousands of people genuine hardship and would later be estimated to have cost the federal government about five billion dollars. While Jacobine didn't understand why so many federal employees should be living paycheck to paycheck—working for the feds had generally been a good gig for people—she recognized that many people had specific personal situations. If you were a janitor, for example, you weren't very likely to be earning much even though you were working for the federal government.

Likewise if you were one of the people who checked purses and backpacks for weapons and explosives at the entrances to the Smithsonian museums or the National Gallery or the Library of Congress. Even if you were making better money, you might still suddenly find yourself unable to make your rent or mortgage payment. Besides, federal contractors wouldn't get back pay for the shutdown period and countless important functions simply weren't happening at all, such as food inspection, while simultaneously certain groups of government employees were obliged to work unpaid (slavery, in other words). Yet at the same time, Melania Trump was apparently free to fly to her husband's appalling Mar-a-Lago resort in a government plane at taxpayer expense, accompanied by the Secret Service.

So there was no shortage of shady behavior by the Trump administration or for that matter by numerous corporations that paid their employees little or that now felt emboldened to discriminate against gay, lesbian, and trans people; and furthermore, the local Third Women's March was canceled due to weather so Jacobine wasn't marching in that. But one had to proceed with life to the best one was able.

And finally, after thirty-five days in which 380,000 federal workers were furloughed and an additional 420,000 were required to work without knowing in advance when they might next be paid, the shutdown ended.

71

A new major distraction appeared on the scene in February, although to be sure there were many smaller distractions, it seemed, daily. Trump's "fixer" Michael Cohen, who in December had been sentenced to three years in federal prison and ordered to pay a $50,000 fine as a result of committing tax fraud, bank fraud, and campaign finance violations, as well as for having lied to a Senate committee about efforts to build a Trump Tower in Moscow, was finally to testify before Congress. His testimony had been postponed several times, in part due to his alleging that he had received ongoing threats against his family from Trump and Trump's current lawyer Rudy Giuliani. Both had been remarking publicly that Cohen's father-in-law had ties to criminal activity, even to organized crime.

As Cohen's father-in-law had apparently been the one to introduce Cohen to Trump, one might of course surmise that this was where his criminal ties lay...

And on the first day of Cohen's testimony, a closed-door hearing, Florida Republican Congressman Matt Gaetz tweeted, "Hey @MichaelCohen212—Do your wife & father-in-law know about your girlfriends?" and "I wonder if she'll remain faithful when you're in prison. She's about to learn a lot..." This tweet, for which there was no evidence, was widely seen as an attempt to intimidate a witness, but although both the Florida Bar and the House Ethics

Committee investigated Gaetz's tweet, not much happened to him.

Jacobine, who was having her car serviced during the morning of the public hearing, sat in the dealership waiting room watching Cohen testify, an activity which she considered more important than continuing to grade the student papers she had brought along. With Democrats now in charge of the House, perhaps the Trump crime family would finally be cast out of Washington. Jacobine's opinion of Cohen was low, but she was pleased to see that he was making a point of showing documentation to support his new testimony.

He just said, she scrawled, *that he would not accept a pardon from Trump, and says his family has been endangered by the Trump gang. Rep Cummings is cautioning him that he'd better not lie anymore—tell the truth this time since after all he's on his way to prison for perjury.*

Both Democrats and Republicans made frequent reference to Cohen's past lies, but their approaches to this were quite dissimilar. The Democrats focused on warning Cohen not to tell any more lies, whereas the Republicans pretended that he was incapable of telling the truth.

It was tiresome, thought Jacobine, to hear these Republicans waste time asserting that Cohen was a liar. Everyone *knew* he was a liar. Was there likely to be an *honest* person close to Trump who could testify? *These idiots,* she fumed, *seem to think you can't have one crook testify against another.* How else had Mafia figures been investigated in the past? The Democrats were asking real and reasonable questions while the Republicans were just blowing smoke. Was there a single Republican in the lot who had anything useful to say?

Ha, when Gosar calls Cohen a pathological liar, Cohen asks if Gosar means him or Trump. Jacobine didn't think Cohen was a *pathological* liar. Rather, he appeared to be someone who had regularly lied on behalf of his own and Trump's self-interest, which while reprehensible was not exactly pathological. Trump, in her view, was the *pathological* liar. Any truths that emerged from his mouth were surely accidental. Cohen was a strategic liar, which meant he would also be inclined to be truthful when that better served him.

She found Michael Cohen a strange and compelling character. Watching and listening to him, to her surprise Jacobine found herself feeling slightly sympathetic, even sort of liking him, despite regarding his past actions with disdain and disgust. To what extent, she wondered, did her sympathy come from the fact that he was not a bad looking specimen? He didn't look icky like Kushner, Sessions, Gaetz, or most of the other Republican males, nor did he have the kind of fake, glossy, magazine-model look that one could argue Ivanka Trump displayed. Jacobine wasn't sure. But then she realized that she had much the same reaction to Cohen via radio as she had via TV. She had a feeling of "Here's a guy who has been a jerk, a dirt bag, a crook, a sycophant, a liar… but who has hit bottom, is penitent. Sure, he's sorry he got caught, but he seems to be starting to grasp the error of his ways." She thought, *He doesn't seem to be a sociopath like Trump, he seems to care about his family, be genuinely worried about what Trump supporters could do to his kids.* Since Cohen's uncle was a doctor to the Mafia, Cohen definitely had crime-family connections. At the same time, Cohen had been exposed to other ways of life while growing up. Although he had gone to school with other prosperous kids, they would not all have been acquainted with crime in the way you might imagine a kid from a poor neighborhood to have been. Cohen was unquestionably far too fond of money, which had led to his being Trump's nasty pet lawyer for ten years—not to mention his own personal shady business dealings—but that didn't mean he couldn't love his wife and kids and want to protect them as any normal person would. Yet, on the other hand, some of the most powerful Nazis had also shown signs of caring about their families...

Jacobine didn't want to assume that Cohen would genuinely turn his life around, but she believed it was possible. Some people did genuinely reform, and she wanted to believe Cohen would be one. She wasn't making any bets on it, though.

And at a certain point she was jubilant, when prison-bound Cohen pointed out that others who protected Trump would also come to a bad end.

72

As Jacobine and her doctor had been unable to come up with an explanation for the way that she too often awoke nauseated, sometimes feeling as if food was taking an eternity to move out of her stomach, her doctor had now prescribed a gastric emptying test to see just how long it really did take her meals to move along. This test would involve eating a slightly radioactive snack and then having periodic images made with a gamma camera to see how quickly the radioactive material proceeded toward the gut.

Jacobine prepared for her test by ordering a large breakfast at a popular eatery near the hospital, as she wouldn't be allowed to eat or drink after half-past nine. She'd been slightly unsure whether Daisies would be open, as she'd read recently that one of its founders had been found dead of an overdose in the restaurant office, but the place seemed to be hopping all the same, so she just hoped they'd bring her omelet quickly. She'd meant to get up at seven and have a leisurely breakfast, but she'd ended up watching footage of the Cohen testimony until after midnight, as she hadn't been able to watch all of it live, and that had caused her to oversleep.

The technician mixed the radioactive tracer with an egg and scrambled it to make a rather dry little sandwich, which made Jacobine wish she had not had an omelet for breakfast; this was not an appealing egg at all when she had had three tastier ones just hours before. She choked down the mixture, however, and lay down in the posture required for the initial scan. After that, she could lie there and read her book until the next scan, and again until the next, and again until two hours had passed, at which point the technician allowed her to depart holding a paper that explained she would be mildly radioactive for the next few days. It had been a rather uneventful procedure but not, apart from the less than appealing egg sandwich, unpleasant. She had been able to read quite a few pages of Muriel Spark's *Loitering with Intent* during that two-hour period, which had indeed made the experience fairly relaxing and enjoyable.

73

Meanwhile, a new cafe had opened in Jacobine's neighborhood, so she was giving it some support by going there to work when she didn't need to be on campus. Whether that would continue to be a good plan, she was unsure. Was the cafe attracting a particular set of customers that, while perfectly all right in themselves, would not be conducive to Jacobine's work? This remained to be seen, but Jacobine's first and second visits indicated that during the week it was heavily populated by families with toddlers, which was decidedly not to her taste as an adult trying to work.

It was odd, too, to observe some of the interactions at the counter. For instance, on Jacobine's first visit, she had brought her own mug, but the worker had poured her coffee first into a paper cup, then from there into the mug, and then threw out the paper cup. Um—was this person unclear on the concept of a travel mug preventing waste of resources, or was she merely a little frazzled?

Then there had been the customer who for some reason said she wanted only the *froth* from the espresso machine. This situation quickly escalated. First, the barista had tried pouring—but if you poured, the froth poured last after the liquid milk. There then followed a long discussion, in which the customer was soon stating that it didn't matter, whatever they did was okay with her, while the staff, in an attempt to provide stellar customer service, was claiming that they wanted to learn how to offer froth on its own, and so, against the customer's wishes, they were throwing out all of the unsuccessful attempts.

Next, a different customer poured herself some half-and-half only to realize that, *OMG*, as there was only one container on the counter, maybe it wasn't nondairy "alternative milk!" This resulted in the staff once again throwing out a cup of coffee; they offered up a choice of almond milk or oat milk (apparently soy milk had gone out of fashion and was no longer the standard alternative milk?), and the customer was surprised to learn that they didn't have *coconut milk* but she was curious about the *oat milk*...

All of this made Jacobine feel like shouting "First World Problems!"—which was not a criticism she typically lobbed at anyone, since wherever you lived, you had a particular set of possible problems and it wasn't actually dreadful for North Americans to complain just because their electricity went out or because it was expensive to fix their cars or whatever. But this—well, what about all the people around the world but also *right here in town* who didn't have decent access to nutritious food and drink? You could bet that they were not throwing out their coffee, assuming they had any, on the grounds that they only wanted the froth from the espresso machine or that (even if they couldn't digest dairy milk) they wanted alternative milk instead of half-and-half.

On the other hand, Jacobine was sympathetic to the young teacher who settled down to grade, opened her laptop, asked for the Wi-Fi code, and was told that the café didn't have Wi-Fi yet. These days one did expect a café to have Wi-Fi, although as the place hadn't yet been open a week, Jacobine didn't really fault the establishment on this.

And if you did have Wi-Fi, then, if you happened to make the mistake of looking at Facebook in the midst of working, you were likely—or at least Jacobine was likely—to be assailed with advertisements asserting "National shapewear day is here!" and "Say goodbye to under breast sweat," claiming "This bra is perfect for my large breasts!" or telling one all about "The thigh saver short" or exhorting one to "Save $3 on the #1 brand for Light Bladder Leaks!" Jacobine might be nearly sixty, but she had not the slightest interest in any of this. No sirree, not even though she had gone from a AA-cup bra to a C-cup and her bladder was not quite as well controlled as it had been two or three years ago.

74

And then came further terrible, terrible news—although in these times perhaps not so surprising—there had been a massacre in the mosques of Christchurch, New Zealand. At least forty people had been killed, with many more injured. There was absolute mayhem. Jacobine was in tears.

Yet then, working at her favorite of the local cafés she could hear a professional-looking woman of about her own age advising a young Muslim "mentee" in hijab about the importance of keeping her GPA up, as well as what the girl could do "at your church... at your church, your synagogue..." The mentee politely said "mosque"...

Jacobine was just cringing.

Fortunately, as the conversation continued, it became clear that the two had actually known each other for years—perhaps through the Big Sister program or something like that—and they knew each other's families and friends. Well, that was a relief. So while the older woman's faux pas was astonishing and in fact was even more surprising given her evident years of involvement with a Muslim family, it at least couldn't have thrown the high school student completely. But still, what a day to make such a mistake...

And then New Zealanders came together in support of their Muslims and rejected the Australian shooter who had written a manifesto stating he supported Trump as "a symbol of renewed white identity and common purpose." Their Prime Minister, who had just attended a school rally participating in the day's Global Climate Strike, cancelled her remaining public appearances for the day and directed that flags on "all Government and public buildings" should be flown at half-mast until further notice.

A few days later, US Special Counsel Robert Mueller submitted his long-awaited report on Russian interference into the 2016 election to the Attorney General, who then sent Congress a letter summarizing its conclusions in a manner that Mueller privately objected led to "public confusion." It would be another month before a redacted version of the report, which did "not exonerate" the president, was released.

75

Jacobine hadn't seen or spoken with Cinda since just after New Year's, and while she felt slightly guilty about that, especially when Kerry mentioned that one of Cinda's dogs had unexpectedly died, all the same she was rather enjoying not having to listen to every last detail about the dogs and about how awful it was working under Kyle.

But when Cinda called, Jacobine figured she should answer. After all, just because Cinda could talk endlessly didn't mean they weren't still friends. Jacobine supposed it could even be seen as karma for all the times she herself had talked endlessly on the phone to various patient friends, long ago in her twenties when there were numerous life questions to be figured out, mostly relating to unrequited love—either her own or that of others for her. She recognized that she had often waxed repetitive back then when pondering these problems from every angle she could think of.

"How are things with you?" asked Jacobine politely.

"Oh, things are pretty good for the most part," claimed Cinda; but before long she proceeded to contradict this assertion. "I can't believe it's been a year since we talked!" she lamented.

Jacobine gasped at this strange assertion and said "It hasn't been anything like a year, because we saw each other right after New Year's. We went ice skating and saw that textile exhibition."

"Oh, that's right," said Cinda, "I guess we did see each other then."

And a fair number of other times during the past year, thought Jacobine.

Cinda then further startled Jacobine by announcing that she was looking forward to teaching at Jacobine's university the next year. In the fall, Jacobine's department chair had been eager to firm up some sabbatical replacement courses, so after Cinda had expressed initial interest, Jacobine had emailed Cinda to confirm that she was interested in offering a museum studies course, and Cinda had replied that she had to check with Kyle. Jacobine and her chair had heard nothing further from Cinda, so Mark had made other arrangements.

Cinda seemed quite surprised to hear that Jacobine's department had already sewn up the next year's schedule without including her. "But I got the okay from Kyle!" she exclaimed.

"That's all very well, but you didn't tell me or Mark," said Jacobine. "Mark's already hired someone else."

"But it's so early!" cried Cinda. "It's only March!"

"Mark wrapped this up months ago," said Jacobine, who had been annoyed not to hear back from Cinda after making the effort to recruit her. "He doesn't like to wait around on this kind of thing."

"But I had all kinds of ideas for how I was going to teach the course this time," said Cinda. "I was going to take the students to a different museum each week to meet with the staff. I can't believe you've gone ahead and hired someone else already." She seemed quite offended that Jacobine's department might already have put together the schedule without her.

"Well, we didn't hear back from you. I'm sorry, but that's just how it is."

There was a slight pause. "Well, you know I haven't had any way to reach you now that you don't have a cell phone," asserted Cinda.

Jacobine was staggered anew. After the loss and theft of her cell phone during her conference trip the previous fall, she had not seen any pressing need to replace it. "I have email and a landline, not to mention a phone on my desk at work, so you shouldn't have any trouble reaching me!" After all, while there were a few people who had only had her old cell number, Cinda wasn't one of them.

"I don't find those to be satisfactory ways of reaching you," said Cinda in self-righteous tones. "I'd rather call you on your cell phone. When I call your landline I always hang up without leaving a message."

"What on earth is the point of that?" demanded Jacobine. "How am I supposed to know you even called?"

"I don't like to leave messages," claimed Cinda, although she had, in the past, left no shortage of messages on both phones.

Jacobine took a deep breath. "I'm not usually near enough to pick up the phone before the machine picks up," she pointed out. "But at least I know where to find my home phone. I never had the faintest idea where my cell phone was. In any case, I screen my calls because there are so many robocalls. I have to see the number or hear a message before I'll pick up."

"That's part of why I got rid of my landline," said Cinda, "there were all those robocalls on it."

Yes, thought Jacobine, *you prefer to talk for hours on end on a cell phone that drops the call multiple times during each conversation!* She said, "I have Caller ID, so I can pick up calls from people I know. That's why I answered your call today! And I can usually get to the home phone by the time the machine starts, whereas the cell phone would usually ring about twelve times while I tried to figure out where it was, or I dropped it when pulling it out of my bag or I accidentally hit some button that ended the call before I could answer."

Cinda continued to assert that she would not have left a message on Jacobine's landline had Jacobine not happened to pick up the phone, because she didn't like landlines and besides, she didn't like to email because she didn't like using her computer at home and her tablet wasn't useful for email because she didn't like typing on it, and she couldn't reach Jacobine via email anyway.

"I have two email addresses and you know both of them," said Jacobine. "It's possible I may at some point have missed seeing an email from you, but generally speaking I respond to emails pretty quickly."

"Well, I don't think you've missed answering any emails from me, because I don't send emails anymore except for work," said Cinda.

"Fine," said Jacobine, "then I'm glad I haven't missed anything, but all the same you can't claim you have no way of reaching me, because I have a home phone with Caller ID and an answering machine and I have two email accounts."

Jacobine wondered if she could get this call to end short of hanging up and pretending the call had been dropped. As Cinda's phone typically dropped calls every few minutes, it was unusual that there had been no interruptions yet.

But Cinda seemed to unravel further as the call went on. "I'm only staying at the museum until I turn sixty-five and can get Medicare," she announced. "But if Kyle keeps being such a piss-poor boss, I might leave before then even if I haven't lined up a new job."

"What about your health insurance in the meantime? Trump keeps trying to get rid of the Affordable Care Act, after all."

"If Trump removes the requirement to have insurance, then I just won't have any."

"He's actually already done that. The 'individual mandate' is gone. But what if something happens to you?" asked Jacobine.

"Well, I don't want to linger, so it wouldn't matter if I didn't have insurance," said Cinda, as if this were only obvious.

"What if it's not something life-threatening?" said Jacobine. "What if it's just something that would be expensive without insurance, like breaking a hip?"

"Why go on living if my health isn't good enough to go hiking and camping?"

"Oh, come on, people get hip replacements all the time and lead normal lives afterward. Besides, that's just an example. What if something else happened to you? What if you had a bout of pneumonia or developed gout or broke your wrist next time the dogs drag you downhill on a trail?"

"Well, I would just have to die anyway, because Trump is destroying America and if he succeeds, there won't be any reason to stick around."

Jacobine had no rejoinder for this.

"But," said Cinda, "that hasn't happened yet. In the meantime there's a lot of traveling I want to do. I just need to come up with travel partners for some of it." She began to talk about all of the places she wanted to go before she died—Peru, China, Japan, the Galapagos, England, Alaska—and what sort of adventure camping groups she might be able to find that were not insanely expensive—and which trips Jacobine really needed to join her on—

Jacobine admitted to herself that she was probably becoming a trifle irritating herself, because when she wasn't muttering "Yes" and "uh huh" and "oh" she was pushing back on some of this stuff. She was afraid that most of what Cinda was saying just seemed ridiculous to her. But she thought that while she herself might be compounding the irritation factor, this conversation really made her feel like Cinda was just losing it.

"We ought to get together," said Cinda next, "but May and June will be extra busy for me."

This made no sense to Jacobine as it was not even the end of March yet.

It was all very strange. Jacobine wanted to be a charitable person, but she found it hard to be her best self in this sort of conversation.

•   •   •

A few days later, Jacobine's phone rang. She knew it was Cinda—while Cinda's name never showed on the caller ID, fortunately her area code was not one favored by robocallers and so Jacobine could identify her calls by area code. Jacobine had left Cinda a message at five o'clock that afternoon, but now it was eleven and Cinda wasn't leaving a message, while Jacobine had no desire to pick up the phone. Did Cinda really think eleven o'clock at night was a good time to return calls? Surely not... and if something was wrong, Cinda should have left a message.

After their last conversation, Jacobine had begun to wonder if Cinda was becoming deranged. She now didn't call back, as she didn't want to engage in a long call this late at night, although had Cinda been leaving a message when Jacobine got downstairs, Jacobine admittedly would have picked up the phone and spoken with her.

Just before midnight, the phone rang again, displaying the same area code, but this time it rang only once, so this was rather peculiar, even more than the earlier call. Jacobine hoped nothing was truly amiss; Cinda really had to get back to leaving messages!

I have got to find out what Kerry thinks, thought Jacobine. She was meeting Kerry for brunch the next day and she thought Kerry was closer friends with Cinda than she was; they had gotten to know each other through Kerry, really. Besides, Kerry was always sane.

76

Kerry arrived at the restaurant a little after Jacobine. After examining the menu and exclaiming over the difficulty of choosing among the various omelets, scrambles, shrimp-and-grits, huevos rancheros, and forms of pancake, they spent the next few hours on a leisurely brunch, talking about students and teaching and what had inspired them as teens. After a while Jacobine reminded Kerry that she wanted advice on the strange conversation with Cinda.

Kerry said, "Could you review for me just how the conversation went?"

Jacobine obliged.

Kerry said, "If Cinda was sitting outside enjoying the evening, she was probably drinking, and you know Cinda doesn't hold her alcohol well."

Cinda did like her beer, but Jacobine didn't find her any different when she'd had a few drinks than beforehand. Besides, it was March. Cinda was unlikely to be sitting outside enjoying the evening in March. Snow could still be expected at any time.

Jacobine emphasized the miscommunication about courses, and the whole crazy thing about Cinda supposedly being unable to reach her because of her lack of cell phone.

"Would you say that Cinda seemed passive-aggressive?" asked Kerry.

Jacobine said, "Well yes—often, in fact—she's always late, for instance. I stopped asking her to take me to the airport because she'd typically be so late I thought I'd miss my flight, that sort of thing." In the past, when Cinda had lived nearer to Kerry and Jacobine, the three had often taken one another to the airport to avoid paying for cabs and parking. The local airport was small enough that it wasn't necessary to be there hours in advance, but Jacobine was not willing to wait on her porch before dawn wondering whether Cinda had forgotten or overslept or had one of her frequent doggie emergencies.

Jacobine was careful about how she presented all of this, because Cinda and Kerry had always spent a lot of time together and helped each other out, so she didn't know whether Kerry might leap to Cinda's defense. But Kerry's actual response was that Cinda enacted a lot of problematic behaviors generally, not just with Jacobine, and that her friends became her sounding boards.

"She doesn't really stop to learn much about us, she's too busy ignoring and denying her own wounds by taking on loads of activities and talking endlessly about the dogs, her job, and whatever is in front of her at the moment," said Kerry.

Jacobine thought: *Cinda monologs at Kerry just as she does at me, so while Kerry always seems okay with it, I can see where she enjoys a more dialogic conversation with other friends.*

Kerry said, "Cinda doesn't actually know me very well, she doesn't know anything very deep about me as a person. She's not the kind of person I see as being a friend I'd turn to, for instance to talk about anything deeply meaningful if I really needed support. I mean, Cinda never offers an ear or has any real understanding of me, because

Cinda just talks constantly about her own mostly surface concerns."

"I didn't realize you felt that way," said Jacobine. "That's rather sad, that we both feel that way when we know she's lonely and seems to see both of us as important people in her life."

"It is sad," agreed Kerry. "But she brings it upon herself. It took a long time before I really realized how little she listens and to what extent she's just talking to fill a void. I've known her quite a while now. I knew her before she got her current job. And she loses jobs. She's very smart, very capable, but she sabotages herself. She doesn't do something that's required, or she refuses to get along with her boss. I'm not saying it's always all her fault, but there's a pattern. I was on the Board of Trustees where she last worked, and I saw a lot of her, but I had no idea she was about to lose the job until the day before it was announced, when another person mentioned it to me. And as Cinda's friend, it would have been very embarrassing for me if I'd heard it for the first time at the board meeting when everyone else knew already—Cinda hadn't said Word One to me about it, although she knew she'd been put on probation and then hadn't made the necessary changes."

"Oof," said Jacobine.

"Afterwards, I invited Cinda to come over and have comfort food and decompress, but Cinda never even mentioned losing her job, she just chattered endlessly about the dogs and gardening and whatever. And that was so strange for me. She must have been in so much pain, yet she couldn't even mention what had happened even though she knew I knew. So it was a moment of realization for me, to see just how much denial Cinda is constantly in about so many parts of her life. That even when a friend offers comfort at a painful time, she's not facing the fact that a sad thing happened to her which was *her own fault* and was no surprise to anyone who knew what was going on, because at a certain point there wasn't any chance of negotiation, there was no wiggle room, no going back."

"That's a very sad story," said Jacobine. "I had heard about her losing that job—I already knew her then too since I knew her through you—but I didn't know the details. I certainly didn't know that she'd acted like nothing had happened. On the other hand, I can't say I'm really that surprised."

"It must be so hard to go through life like that, constantly repressing your pain when you fail at something. Covering it all with endless trivial chitchat."

"Cinda does just talk about herself most of the time," said Jacobine. "But not in any very insightful way."

"No, I think she just recharges by monologuing to her friends. Meanwhile, we just say 'uh huh' and use the time during her calls to wash the dishes or do the laundry or something."

"Yeah, I do some of that," said Jacobine, "but it's hard to do very much with a phone in one hand."

"We just have to make choices about Cinda's role in our lives, and I've done that," said Kerry.

Jacobine thought Cinda still played a larger role in her own life than seemed desirable, but that could be changed. She didn't need to break with Cinda, but she could scale back contact. Surely there were other people at the university, or in town, who might be more interesting bike partners, or who didn't insist on bringing dogs along on hikes to distract one from noticing small mushrooms and mosses, or who even might want to hear about her own research and photographic projects and museum exhibitions now and then. She knew some interesting people in the area, she just didn't know most of them all that well. And it occurred to her, as well, that perhaps Cinda's odd behavior stemmed at least in part from stress, the stress of living during the Trump presidency. Perhaps, post-Trump and post-retirement, Cinda might recover some degree of normalcy.

77

For her sixtieth birthday, Jacobine went to visit her mother, who now lived some hours away in Maryland in an appealing one-bedroom apartment filled with plants and mementoes. Jacobine's mother remained for the most part in good mental and physical health, although as was to be expected neither was quite what it had been ten years earlier. After going for lunch at a nearby Thai restaurant, they sat talking in the living room, where Jacobine's mother pointed out the locations where she had had various small skin cancers removed from her face during the past year.

"I must say they did a very good job," she commented. "I can hardly even find most of the scars anymore."

Jacobine agreed that for the most part the scars were not noticeable, or at least were really only discernible if you were actually looking for them.

"And I'm certainly glad to be done with those cataract operations," said Jacobine's mother. "Having those spread out over six months was really too much. They should have scheduled the second one for immediately after the first one had healed!"

"That's true," said Jacobine. "But at least now they're over and healed and you can move on to getting a hearing aid." This was something they had discussed at various times in recent years and Jacobine's mother had indicated that she would get the hearing aid after having the cataracts taken care of.

"I'm going to wait till summer's over to do that," announced Jacobine's mother now.

"What?" exclaimed Jacobine. "Why on earth would you do that?"

"It's too hot out to get a hearing aid right now."

"That doesn't make any sense at all! There's no reason to wait to get a hearing aid. You'll be much happier when you have one, and they always say you shouldn't wait too long to get one. It's not just that you'd hear better, they've found that people with hearing loss start to lose brain function because they aren't hearing everything that they should. When the brain doesn't receive certain types of stimuli, it gives up processing them. People who spend too long in total darkness end up blind, for instance. And I heard an interview with a guy whose taste buds disappeared because he wasn't medically able to eat using his mouth for a long time. You don't want to wait any longer on this, because the longer you wait, the harder it'll be to get used to having the hearing aids."

"Oh, I'll get tested again, but I wonder whether I should get tested at both Kaiser and Costco." Jacobine's mother's health insurance was through Kaiser Permanente and she was a devotee of the Costco membership stores, where she routinely purchased gallons of milk and orange juice and startlingly large quantities of fruit.

"I don't see any reason that you'd need to be tested twice," asserted Jacobine. "I'm sure you can take the prescription from Kaiser, and Costco will be glad to fill it, just like with your glasses."

"It might be interesting to see what they both say, though," said her mother.

"I don't think there's any need to do that," returned Jacobine, who was becoming tired of this topic. "The main thing is that you need to get a hearing aid and stop putting it off. We should call Kaiser this afternoon and get moving on this. You'll be much happier once you have the hearing aid. There's no point in living with diminished faculties if you don't have to."

"I suppose," said her mother mildly, and adroitly changed the subject. "Now how is *your* health? Have you been to the doctor lately?"

"My health is about as usual," said Jacobine; "it's pretty good and I see the doctor regularly. I saw the doctor just last week."

"What did you see him about?" inquired her mother with keen interest.

"Oh, just my arthritis," said Jacobine, not seeing any point in revealing that she had now also been diagnosed with a mysterious case of gastroparesis, given that in her case this did not seem to be a harbinger of impending death or great misery.

"Your arthritis!" exclaimed her mother. "Is that bothering you again?"

"Well, you know that it does from time to time."

"Where does it bother you?"

Jacobine sighed, as she felt her arthritis had been a significant enough topic of conversation between them in recent years that she should not have to detail it yet again. "It's still just my one hip."

"What did the doctor have to say?"

"He gave me five days' worth of Prednisone and we're going to try a different painkiller."

Jacobine's mother took on an increasingly animated appearance. "You should be sure to take that turmeric I gave you. It did wonders for me!"

Jacobine said, "I do take it. Not every day, but I do take it. I told you the orthopedist recommended it, too."

"Did he?" said her mother, victorious. "I really think it is a wonder drug."

"Yes, she said it was one of the things I could do to put off getting a hip replacement."

"A hip replacement!" exclaimed her mother then. "Are you going to need a hip replacement?"

"Eventually," said Jacobine patiently. "We've known this for the past year. I don't suppose I'll need one for at least ten years, though."

"A hip replacement!" repeated her mother. "Goodness!" She pondered this appalling but old news for a moment and then said "Would it help if you lost some weight?"

Jacobine restrained herself and said "I don't know. Maybe, but I doubt it would make much difference."

"You should really lose some weight," proclaimed her mother. "You've gotten very heavy, and you'd look much better if you lost some weight. You really need to get your weight under control."

This was beyond what Jacobine was willing to put up with. "That's ridiculous," she said in scathing tones. "My weight *is* under control. It's always within a given range, which is a fairly narrow range. Sometimes it's at the high end of that range. Just because I prefer it to be at the lower end of that range does not mean it's out of control when it's at the higher end. I normally eat small meals of healthy foods, and I'd have to start living on greens alone if I were going to take in a lot fewer calories."

"You'd still look a lot better if you lost some weight," persisted her mother, who had rarely remarked upon Jacobine's weight prior to Jacobine's menopause but who now sailed boldly into these waters at least once a year.

"I am not fat," stated Jacobine severely, "and my looks do not vary all that much between when I weigh more and when I weigh less. People are not disgusted or offended by the way I look—" she was well aware that most people considered her fairly slender, but she did not care to make comparisons—"and it's perfectly normal for people to gain a little weight in middle age; animals do this too and then they usually lose it when they get old."

"I weigh 123, and I could lose a few pounds," claimed Jacobine's mother.

Jacobine could feel her eyes rolling ceiling-ward. "You don't need to lose a few pounds, you've just got a little flab where you used to have muscle. That's normal for a person your age, but if you don't like it you could start lifting weights along with doing your stretches."

"On a different topic," said her mother brightly, "I don't know what I'm going to do when that pine in the window gets much bigger."

"Your Norfolk pine," pronounced Jacobine, "is not yet a foot tall and your ceiling is at least eight feet high, so as Norfolk pines don't grow all that fast indoors, I don't think this is going to become a problem in your lifetime."

• • •

On her way home from her mother's, Jacobine stopped to visit a friend who lived midway. Ten or so years earlier, she and Ira had enjoyed a fairly torrid affair, which for various reasons mostly beyond Jacobine's control had soon been transmuted into a friendship that sometimes still featured, now and then at unpredictable intervals, the benefits appropriate to still-torrid affairs. On this occasion they had arranged to go out to dinner.

Ira was sitting on the front porch of his cottage when she arrived, enjoying the slight breeze and relative lack of mosquitoes. At her approach, he arose and they embraced warmly, at length.

"It's good to see you," she said as they uncoupled.

"Likewise," he said. "Shall we take in your bags?"

"Yes, I suppose we should," she said, not that there was much to take in. She had intended to bring him a bottle of gin, but had become distracted on the way and forgotten to buy one.

After many years of driving everywhere, Ira had discovered the pleasures of public transit and computer-optimized ride services, so with a flourish he brought forth his phone from some inner pocket and proceeded, wordlessly, to schedule them a ride to the restaurant. Unlike Jacobine, he had been one of the early adopters of the smartphone, and throughout their acquaintance he had forever been finding new uses for the device. She found this mildly amusing, but recognized that he employed his phone much more skillfully, and for the most part unobtrusively, than almost anyone else she knew.

At the restaurant they drank their gin and contemplated the menu in a leisurely manner between visits from their server, who was eager to make herself useful. Ira took a serious interest in food and liked to know things such as which restaurants made their own charcuterie and which bars grew their own herbs to make aromatics and bitters. He was inclined to order entrees featuring meats whereas Jacobine was inclined to avoid these in favor of entrees featuring beets or squash or potentially some sort of fish. Eventually, in this case, he settled on duck and she chose a crepe with mushrooms. The server clearly felt that Jacobine should augment her choice with one or two other small plates, but Jacobine observed that she could always order more after the crepe, should she so desire. As she had pointed out to her mother, she was not generally a heavy eater.

"I might actually have room for dessert if I only order one of the small plates," she said to Ira.

"I don't plan on having dessert," said Ira, "but don't let that stop you from having one. We're celebrating your birthday, after all."

"I almost never want a dessert," said Jacobine, "but now and then it makes a nice change to have one."

"How's your mother?" asked Ira. Neither had ever met the other's mother, but over the years each had heard a certain amount about these maternal parents. Jacobine saw much more of her mother than Ira saw of his, as hers lived closer and unlike Ira she did not make a practice of avoiding her family.

"She's doing well enough," said Jacobine. "She's in decent health, she's still competent to live on her own, and she keeps busy with different projects. On the other hand, she began telling me that I needed to lose weight, which was annoying."

"You don't need to lose weight," said Ira firmly. "You are exactly the right weight and shape."

"I'd prefer to lose a few pounds, but there's nothing necessary about it, so there's no excuse for her to go on about it."

"You are exactly the right weight and shape," repeated Ira, "and I'd be happy to write her a letter telling her so."

Jacobine smiled. "I don't think that will be necessary. She only gets on this kick about once a year. A year from now I might weigh ten pounds less and she might still think I need to lose weight. Or she might tell me I look much better. There's no way to predict it."

Ira said, "My mother tells me I need to lose weight too. She's right, but it's none of her business, so I ignore her."

"How is she?" inquired Jacobine.

"Well, as you know, I avoid seeing her during the majority of the year, so my encounters with her are usually at Thanksgiving. She was in fine fettle last Thanksgiving, and according to my sister that's still the case. She enjoys her life and I enjoy mine, and so long as our lives don't intersect too frequently, all's well. She has an apartment of her own at one of those senior living facilities, and I gather that she has an active social life there. Since the notion of an active social life is utterly abhorrent to me, I prefer to leave her to her own devices."

Jacobine was aware that Ira's abhorrence of the idea of an active social life did not prevent him from holding occasional small dinner parties, attending the funerals of his co-workers, or learning the names of his favorite bartenders. He was merely particular about the humans with whom he socialized. Jacobine too was particular about the humans with whom she socialized, but she was less rigorous about it than was Ira.

When they returned from the restaurant, they sat upon Ira's couch and wrapped themselves together in a relatively stable mass, like a more complex version of yin and yang, and quietly remained that way for a long time before rising and venturing upstairs. Ira did not steer Jacobine toward the guest bedroom as he sometimes did, so they threw off their clothing and crawled onto his large bed, where he pulled Jacobine atop himself and they began to reacquaint themselves with the feel of each other's skin and the shape of each other's bodies.

It was a nice way to turn sixty, thought Jacobine.

Acknowledgements

There are always many people who deserve thanks in the making of a book. This novel benefitted from all the friends, family, colleagues, and neighbors who helped me stay somewhat sane during the Trump presidency, even though the period was equally stressful for many of them. Particular thanks go, however, to Dirk van Nouhuys and Kathleen White, who kindly read the manuscript when it was done and offered their comments. I also want to thank Reagan Rothe and the rest of the Black Rose team for their faith in this book, and the members of my current writing group for their support on new works in progress. By the time this book sees print, I know I'll owe thanks to many other people as well! John Smalley, Moazzam Sheik, and César Love, too, have been stalwart supporters of my writing.

About the Author

Karla Huebner has lived on a boat and worked in factories, offices, theater, publishing, oil refineries, private investigation, and adolescent drug rehab; she eventually taught Art History at Wright State University in Dayton, Ohio. Her short fiction has appeared in such places as the *Northwest Review, Colorado State Review, Magic Realism, Fantasy Macabre, Weave*, and *Opossum*, and her collection *Heartwood* was a finalist for the 2020 Raz-Shumaker award. Her books include the novel *In Search of the Magic Theater* (Regal House) and the prize-winning study *Magnetic Woman: Toyen and the Surrealist Erotic* (University of Pittsburgh Press). Like Cinda and Jacobine, she enjoys hiking, biking, and canoeing.

Note from the Author

Word of mouth is crucial for any author to succeed. If you enjoyed *Too Early to Know Who's Winning*, please leave a review online—anywhere you are able. Even if it's just a sentence or two. It would make all the difference and would be very much appreciated.

Thanks!
Karla Huebner

We hope you enjoyed reading this title from: